"Will undoubtedly draw comparisons to the titular
character in Beverly Cleary's Ramona series.
An engaging series opener about the power of truth
to moor and free even the sulkiest of souls."
—*Kirkus Reviews*, starred review

"With its short chapters, lively occasional illustrations
by Ho, and energetic feuds between Harriet's
cat and her grandmother's beloved basset hound,
this series opener is a winner."
—*Publishers Weekly*, starred review

"A gentle, slow-moving summer adventure
that's big on character growth."
—*School Library Journal*

"The versatile Elana K. Arnold, author of the
A Boy Called Bat trilogy, offers a memorable portrait
of a child navigating changes in her life in this
charming illustrated mystery."
—*Buffalo News*

Also by Elana K. Arnold

The Bat Chronicles:

A Boy Called Bat

Bat and the Waiting Game

Bat and the End of Everything

The House That Wasn't There

Just Harriet

Elana K. Arnold
With drawings by Dung Ho

WALDEN POND PRESS
An Imprint of HarperCollinsPublishers

Walden Pond Press is an imprint of HarperCollins Publishers.

Just Harriet

Text copyright © 2022 by Elana K. Arnold

Illustrations copyright © 2022 by Dung Ho

Library of Congress Cataloging-in-Publication Data

Names: Arnold, Elana K., author. | Ho, Dung, illustrator.

Title: Just Harriet / Elana K. Arnold ; with drawings by Dung Ho.

Description: First edition. | New York, NY : Walden Pond Press, an
imprint of HarperCollins Publishers, [2022] | Audience: Ages
6-10. | Audience: Grades 2-3. | Summary: Harriet Wermer
is unhappy about having to spend her summer with her
grandmother on Marble island until she discovers a mystery
involving her dad from when he was a boy living on the island.

Identifiers: LCCN 2021021314 | ISBN 978-0-06-309205-1 (pbk.)

Subjects: CYAC: Mystery and detective stories. | Grandmothers—
Fiction. | Family life—Fiction. | LCGFT: Novels.

Classification: LCC PZ7.A73517 Ju 2022 | DDC [Fic]—dc23

LC record available at https://lccn.loc.gov/2021021314

Typography by Molly Fehr

22 23 24 25 26   PC/CWR   10 9 8 7 6 5 4 3 2 1

First paperback edition, 2023

For Jordan Brown,
my editor and friend

Contents

1. Things You Should Know _____ 1

2. Not Spying _____ 10

3. On the Way to Nanu's House _____ 18

4. Welcome to Marble Island _____ 28

5. Harriet's Hideaway _____ 38

6. Don't Cry _____ 45

7. Tip Troller _____ 56

8. Nanu's Shed _____ 67

9. Hans & Gretchen's Ice Cream Parlor _____ 78

10. Bubble Machine _____ 90

11. A Keyhole, a Key _____ 99

12. Island Loggerhead Shrikes _____ 115

13. Another Mystery _____ 124

14. Moneypenny's Constitutional _____ 131

15. Inside Sounds and Outside Sounds _____ 140

16. Behind the Door _____ 154

17. The Gingerbread House _____ 164

18. Mabel Marble _____ 176

Acknowledgments _____ 197

1

Things You
Should Know

MY NAME IS HARRIET WERMER.

There are some things you should know about me before I tell you everything else.

Let's start with the worst things first.

Sometimes I lie. I don't know why I lie, and it's usually about dumb things that people figure out right away, or really soon. It's embarrassing, if you want to know the truth. (The truth about lying! Hahaha.)

I have loads of nightmares. Really bad ones, so bad they're called night terrors. Trust me. They're awful. Usually, they're about falling. I hate falling.

Okay, fine. This last one I wasn't going to admit, even to you, but then I figured, I might as well be honest for a change. Sometimes, when I'm having a night terror, I pee my bed.

That last one is the one that most kids like to tease me about, when they find out. I don't tell people about it, usually. It's one of those things that's on a need-to-know basis, and as far as I'm concerned, it's not something *anyone* needs to know.

But it's weird how people find stuff out anyway.

Oh. That leads me to one last thing. Sometimes, when I get mad or embarrassed—like if I get caught telling a lie or when someone finds out about me peeing in my bed, I get a little . . . well, Mom calls it "out of hand."

On the last day of third grade, which happened

not very long ago, I guess I got "out of hand." But it wasn't my fault. Not to start with, anyway.

Maybe you should know just *one* more thing about me. Mom really did name me after Harriet the Spy, that character from a book. It was her favorite book when she was a kid, and she'd always known that when she grew up, if she had a daughter, she'd name her daughter Harriet.

But whenever anyone says to me, "Hey, your name's Harriet! Like Harriet the Spy!" I stop them right there and say:

"No. It's just Harriet."

"Okay, Just Harriet," the grown-ups *always* say. (It's like they've all read the same handbook called *Dumb Grown-Up Jokes*.)

That's why sometimes the kids call me Just Harriet. Because they heard our teacher, Mrs. Robinson, make that joke on the first day of third grade, and it stuck. Grown-ups don't seem to get that a thing like a nickname can follow a person for a long time. I don't understand; weren't grown-ups kids, before they were grown-ups? Do they all get, like, grown-up amnesia or something?

When I grow up, I'm not going to forget how icky and uncomfortable and . . . infuriating it can be to be a kid. That's a promise.

Anyway, like I was telling you, sometimes I lie, and sometimes I pee my bed, and sometimes I have night terrors. But I'll bet there are some things about you that you're not so fond of. My Nanu likes to say, "Everyone's got something." Nanu is pretty smart. She's my dad's mom, and she lives on an island. But I'll tell you more about her later.

First, I want to tell you about that thing that happened on the last day of third grade. It didn't actually have much to do with school at all.

Dad picked me up, and that was the first thing that was weird. Almost always, Mom is the one to take me to school and pick me up after, because she can do her job from home and Dad has to travel a lot. I don't really love it when I'm expecting things to go one way but instead something else happens. If it were up to me, things wouldn't be *changing* all the time. So even though I was glad to see Dad, I had been expecting to see Mom. And maybe that started my rotten mood right there.

So yeah, Dad picked me up when school was over. He didn't even want to stop for a special last-day-of-school drink at my favorite coffee shop, Doug's Drive-Thru De-Lite.

"But it's a last-day-of-school tradition," I told him. "Every year since kindergarten, Mom has taken me to Doug's on the last day of school and we get a special drink."

"Not this time," Dad said. "Mom's at the doctor, and we need to go pick her up."

Mom had been having lots of doctor's appointments because of the *pregnancy*. I hadn't particularly wanted a little brother, but no one asked me.

Because if they had, I'd have told them that three is the perfect number for a family. Three is my favorite number. At first I ignored all the talk about the baby and all the baby stuff they were buying and piling up in Mom's office. But Mom's belly kept getting bigger and bigger, and that was harder to ignore. And now, apparently, Marson Wermer was due to be born on August eleventh.

(They did ask me about the name, but they didn't listen to my opinion. There was still time, though, to change their minds.)

"We can go through the drive-through on the way to the doctor's," I said. "Please? It's a tradition."

"It's not on the way," Dad said.

We were in the car, but we were still in the school parking lot, stuck in a long line waiting to get out.

"You guys said the baby wouldn't change anything, and now it's changing the last-day-of-school tradition," I said.

Dad sighed. It was the sigh that meant that he was going to change his mind. And I was right. He drove to Doug's Drive-Thru De-Lite. I got a strawberry-vanilla smoothie with extra whipped cream. Then we drove to the doctor's office.

Mom's baby doctor's office was in the same building as my pediatrician's. Dad let me wait in the courtyard by the koi pond while he went inside. He could see me the whole time through the window next to the door. I saw Mom waiting for us in the reception area. She waved at me.

I waved back.

I was surprised when she didn't stand up. It turned out she was sitting in a wheelchair. Dad pushed her to the door. For a second I couldn't see them, and then the door opened and out they came.

"Hey, baby," Mom said. She looked tired. She had dark marks under her eyes, and her hair was sort of in a bun but also sort of in a ponytail. "You got a smoothie!"

"Last-day-of-school tradition," Dad said.

I gulped a big slurp of the smoothie. It got stuck for a minute in my throat when I got nervous that maybe Mom would tell Dad that there was no last-day-of-school smoothie tradition.

But even though she raised her eyebrows, she didn't say anything about the lie. We walked together back to the car. Well, Mom didn't walk. She rolled.

After Dad helped Mom get into the front seat, he went around to the back of the car and put the wheelchair into the trunk. I didn't like knowing that it was back there, coming home with us to our house. I didn't ask about why Mom was in a wheelchair. But it wasn't because I didn't *care*. It's because I already knew that it wasn't good, whatever the reason was.

I slurped furiously on the smoothie. But it didn't taste very good anymore.

2

Not Spying

THE LAST DAY OF SCHOOL is supposed to be a great day. But before Dad picked me up it had only been an okay day, and after he picked me up, it got worse and worse.

When we got home, Dad took the wheelchair out of the trunk and opened it next to Mom's side of the car. Mom said, "I don't need to be pushed, it's not far to the house," but Dad said, "Doctor's orders," and so Mom climbed into the seat.

"I want to push her," I said, but Dad wouldn't let me. If you asked me, he was being awfully bossy. Telling Mom she had to sit in the wheelchair and telling me I couldn't be the one to push it. There were three steps up to the front porch, and Mom had to walk up these. Then Dad got the chair up the stairs and she sat down again.

"Open the door, Harriet," Dad said.

He didn't say *please*, so I just stood there waiting.

"Harriet, I'm not in the mood," he said.

It was true, he *didn't* look "in the mood." So I opened the door. I didn't even complain very much when he rolled over my foot with one of the wheelchair tires.

"Sorry, baby," Mom said.

Then he took her straight to their bedroom. My cat, Matzo Ball, was being adorable, asleep in his kitten position on Mom's pillow. That was what we called it, the way he liked to curl up with his

little head tucked between his little paws—his kitten position. Normally when Matzo Ball was in his kitten position, we all stood around and told him what a good boy he was and admired his long, peachy fuzzy fur. But this time, Dad just grabbed the corner of the pillow and rolled him right off!

"Hey!" I said.

Matzo Ball gave us all one long dirty look, and then he ran out of the room.

"It's not my fault, Matzo Ball!" I called after him. But Matzo Ball didn't listen. "Dad! You need to apologize to Matzo Ball."

"Later, Harriet." He helped Mom out of the wheelchair and into bed. Then he knelt down and untied her sneakers.

"Mom!" I said. "Do you want to see my last-day-of-school celebration dance?"

I didn't really have a last-day-of-school celebration dance. I just started waving my arms around and jumping.

Mom smiled. But she also said, "Later, Harriet."

I stomped out of their room just like Matzo Ball. No one had dumped me off a pillow, but I felt like they had.

Matzo Ball was in the kitchen. He was sitting in a patch of sunlight near the back door, licking his leg. I still felt sorry about the way Dad had treated him, so I got his Good Boy Kitty Num Nums out of the cabinet and shook a few into his bowl. He stopped licking his leg and started chowing down.

I heard Dad close the bedroom door and walk

up the hallway toward the kitchen. I decided that I would be *way too busy* to show him my last-day-of-school celebration dance.

But he didn't ask to see the dance. Instead he walked right past me and out the back door. He took out his phone, sat on the stoop, and called somebody.

"Hey, Mom," he said.

Oh! It was Nanu.

"Yeah, she's okay," he said into the phone. "She's going to have to be on bed rest for a while. Probably until the baby is born."

Bed rest? Like, resting in bed? But it was only June fifth, and the baby wasn't going to be born until August. . . . That was two whole months! No one could stay in bed for two whole months. Not even Matzo Ball, and he *loved* bed.

"Uh-huh," Dad was saying. I wasn't *spying* on him. Not *really*. But I did creep along the floor and poke my head up to look through the little window on the back door.

"So it would be okay if she comes to stay with you? I could bring her out on the ferry tomorrow morning, if that's all right."

Nanu lives on Marble Island. Even though it's an island, it's still part of California, where we live. It's actually not all that far from our house. The only way to get there is on a boat, but it's not too long a boat ride. Usually we visit Nanu every month or so. She comes to see us, too, but only for a week in the fall and another week in the spring; other than that, she's too busy running her bed-and-breakfast, the Bric-a-Brac B&B, to come to what she calls "the mainland." A bed-and-breakfast is like a hotel, except it's inside someone's house. All kinds of tourists who visit Marble Island stay at Nanu's B and B; you never know what sort of people you might meet. I love Nanu and I love the bed-and-breakfast and I love the island.

I burst through the back door. "You can't take Mom to Nanu's for two months," I said. "I won't let you!"

Dad looked up at me. Then he said, "Mom, I'm going to have to call you back." He ended the call, and then he said, "Harriet, honey, I'm not taking your mom to stay with Nanu."

"Good," I said. I folded my arms. I stomped my foot.

"Sweetheart," Dad said, "I don't know how much you heard me say on the phone just now."

"I wasn't spying," I said. Then, "I heard about the bed rest."

Dad nodded. "Mom and the baby are both going to be fine. But her doctor says she needs to take it *really* easy. She's supposed to stay in bed all the time, except to go to the bathroom. And I still have to work. So, you see, there's no one here who can look after you while you're out of school for the summer. And Nanu suggested that it might be a good idea—"

I held up my hand to stop him. "Don't say it." If he didn't say it, maybe it wouldn't be true. I love Nanu and the island more than almost anything, but I didn't love the idea of going there all by myself and staying for two whole months.

"Harriet, honey, you always have fun on Marble Island. And you can help Nanu with the summer season at the bed-and-breakfast."

"You promised the baby wouldn't change *any-thing*," I said.

Dad nodded. "I think probably that was a mistake. I'm sorry about that. Things do change, you know, even if we don't want them to."

I recrossed my arms. I stomped my foot one more time. "I'm not going to Nanu's house," I said. "And that's final."

3

On the Way to Nanu's House

AND THAT WAS WHEN THE last day of school turned into a really rotten day. I freaked out. I stomped. I yelled. I cried.

Eventually I climbed into bed with Mom, and she told me she and Dad didn't like the whole thing any more than I did. "But all of us are just going to have to make the best of a bad situation," she said. And, as always, she was right. Sometimes, no matter what, we have to do things we don't want to do.

At least everyone agreed that I wouldn't be going to Marble Island alone.

The next morning, I explained to Matzo Ball about bad situations, and how we were supposed to make the best of them, but I don't think he was really listening. I knew just how he felt.

Matzo Ball didn't want to be pushed into the carrier.

He didn't want the carrier to be shoved into the car.

He didn't want to wait in line to board the ferry-boat.

But sometimes, even cats have to do things they don't want to do.

I insisted on carrying him myself, even though the carrier was sort of hard to manage. Dad carried everything else.

After Dad stashed my luggage in the racks on

the ferry and we got snacks from the snack bar, we went out to the front deck of the boat. I put Matzo Ball's carrier on the ground between my feet.

Over the intercom, a woman's voice announced, "Thank you for choosing the Starboard Ferry for your journey today! The whole crew is happy to have you aboard. Grown-ups, please keep a close eye on your children. Kids, please keep a close eye on your grown-ups. Lots of goodies and beverages available for purchase at the snack bar! Cash and credit accepted."

There was a staticky sound, and then the voice continued. "Keep your eyes peeled for dolphins and whales! Yesterday's ferry caught sight of three separate pods. Enjoy the ride! We will reach Marble Island in just under forty-five minutes. It's a beautiful day. Smooth waters the whole way."

Then the announcer clicked off and the ferry lurched away from the dock.

I held Matzo Ball's carrier steady with my legs.

He growled. It sounded exactly the way I felt. Growly and unhappy.

The boat was full of tourists going to the island for the day or maybe for a week's vacation. Everyone seemed happy. Kids ran around laughing and playing. Grown-ups sat on the benches and flipped through pamphlets about island activities—snorkeling and fishing and island tours. Since I'd been going to the island all my life, I'd already done all those things.

I decided not to think about how sad it had been to say goodbye to Mom that morning. I decided to focus instead on how Dad hadn't let me get three different kinds of doughnuts at the snack bar on the boat.

"Just choose one," he'd said.

"I should get all three," I argued. "Because you're making me go to Nanu's house."

Dad sighed. "One doughnut. Otherwise you'll get seasick."

I'd chosen powdered sugar. Now, I pulled it out

of its little paper bag. Sugar drifted down like snow-flakes onto the top of Matzo Ball's carrier.

The ferryboat made it past the buoys and started

to pick up speed. Dad stood next to me. He hadn't gotten a snack, just coffee, which he sipped as he looked out at the water. It seemed like he was enjoying the ride. There was nothing good about this boat ride, and I thought it was rude, the way Dad turned his face up to the sun, the way he breathed in deep, the way he didn't seem to even notice how mad I was. To keep myself from yelling at him, I took a bite of my doughnut.

"Meow," said Matzo Ball.

Cold air and salt spray and powdered sugar and doughnut crumbs.

I chewed and swallowed, and even though I'd decided not to think about Mom and saying goodbye, the doughnut formed a lump in my throat and I had to fight back tears. My mad feelings were turning into sad feelings, which was even worse. The mad and the sad mixed together with the doughnut, making me seasick. I took one more bite, but I didn't want the rest. It tasted too sweet, and sort of stale. I threw the second half into the ocean. Maybe the fish would enjoy it.

We were going pretty fast now. Matzo Ball was quiet, like he'd given up. I looked at Dad. He was wearing a blue baseball cap that was almost the same color as his sweatshirt. Blue was his favorite color.

"Hey, kiddo," he said. "I know this wasn't how you planned to spend your summer."

I shook my head. "I was going to go to the city pool and read lots of books and learn how to ride a unicycle."

Actually, I hadn't planned on learning how to ride a unicycle. I don't know why I said that last thing.

Dad grinned. "Well, I don't know if Nanu has a unicycle. She might! Who knows what all is in that shed behind the B and B? She's been stuffing it full of things for years now. You know," he said, "I've always wondered if there might be something amazing in that shed, hidden in among all the knick-knacks and statues and light fixtures and funny old tools. Anything could be in there, really!"

It was true that I'd never explored Nanu's shed, not in all the years I'd been visiting the island. And the thought that there might be interesting things in there made my brain feel tingly, in a good way. But I wasn't about to tell Dad that I was interested. I grunted instead.

"Well," Dad said, "even if there's no unicycle in Nanu's shed, there *is* a city pool on the island. There's also that little library on the other side of town. I used to go there every Saturday when I was a kid. Maybe you can get a card. And there's always the Gingerbread House. . . . That's where the real treasure is. Maybe your Nanu can finally take you there."

I'd never heard of the Gingerbread House, whatever it was. But I could tell Dad wanted me to ask about it, and I wasn't going to give him the satisfaction. I squatted down to check on Matzo Ball. He was in kitten position but with his rear end facing the door. I stuck my fingers through the little gate and gave him a scratch. He ignored me.

I stood up. Then I asked, "Is Mom going to be all right?"

"Yes," said Dad. "She and the baby will both be fine. They just need to rest is all. Take it real easy. That's their job this summer. And my job is to keep going to work so we have money for all the things we need. What's your job, Harriet?"

I rolled my eyes, but Dad wasn't going to move on until I said it. "My job is to help Nanu and keep a Positive Attitude."

"That's right," said Dad.

"And to take care of Matzo Ball," I said.

"I still think we should have left the cat at home," Dad said.

But Dad wasn't the only person who could be

stubborn. If I was going to go live with Nanu for the summer at the Bric-a-Brac B&B on Marble Island, then Matzo Ball would be living there too. Luckily Nanu had agreed.

My sad feelings and my mad feelings were starting to fade a little. I had to admit, it *was* nice out on the open ocean. I turned my face into the wind and felt it almost knock me over. I pushed myself forward, against the wind, and dug in my feet.

Dad put his big warm hand on my shoulder. "That's a strong wind, Harriet," he said. "But you're strong too."

I didn't feel strong up against all that wind, up against a whole summer away from Mom and Dad and home. I didn't think Dad really understood the way I was feeling. Maybe he didn't understand me at all. I grabbed the rail with both of my hands. I held on tight.

4

Welcome to
Marble Island

THE TOURISTS WERE ALWAYS IN a big hurry to get off the ferry as soon as it docked, so Dad and I waited until almost everybody was off the ship before we went to get my luggage. Besides Matzo Ball's carrier, we had brought the really big rolling suitcase, the medium-sized duffel bag, and the small old-fashioned suitcase that I liked to carry books in.

Dad had thought that maybe instead of the

old-fashioned suitcase, I should have used his smaller roller bag. But I liked the suitcase. It had belonged to Dadu—my grandfather—and after he died, I inherited it. It's not all that often that someone inherits something, and I think that if you're lucky enough to inherit a really cool old-fashioned suitcase, and then you have the chance to use it, you should.

Fortunately, Mom agreed with me. "Let her take the suitcase, Walt," Mom had said to Dad that morning before we left for the ferry. "It makes her happy."

The suitcase *did* make me happy. It had stickers all over the front and the back, souvenirs from places Dadu and Nanu had traveled together. I don't actually remember Dadu. He died when I was little. But I liked to trace the words on the stickers on the suitcase and imagine all the places he'd gone. I liked to hold the hard plastic handle, putting my fingers in the little bumpy spots meant for fingers, and imagine his hand holding it in the same way.

But this day, taking the suitcase to Marble Island for the summer, it was too heavy for me to carry. Probably because I'd filled it full of books. And rocks.

They weren't just *any* rocks. They were rocks that I had painted faces on. They were my special collection, and I didn't want to leave them at home. Also they were heavy, and I felt like making Dad carry lots of heavy stuff.

Dad carried the suitcase and the duffel bag and he pulled the big roller bag too. I carried Matzo Ball in his carrier. The carrier had a shoulder strap with a nice pad. It wasn't too heavy for me.

We disembarked—that's a fancy word for getting off a boat—and then we walked up the ramp. Matzo Ball's carrier started to feel heavier, but I didn't complain to Dad. He was huffing and puffing under all the weight from the luggage. I started to think maybe I didn't need to bring *all* the rocks in my collection.

But Dad didn't complain either. That's a good thing about Dad. He's not much of a complainer.

Beep, beep!

There, right on time, was Nanu. She sat behind the steering wheel in her bright-red golf cart. She wore a bright-yellow hat and a bright-green dress and a bright, big smile.

Everything about Nanu was *bright*. Even her wild curly hair, which was brown and silver and gray and white all swirled together.

"There's my Harriet!" she called, and she got out of the golf cart and ran over to give me a big hug. She gave Dad a hug too. "Hello, Walter," she said. "It's so good to see you both."

We loaded my stuff into the tippy back of the golf cart. Then I climbed into the back seat and settled Matzo Ball's carrier next to me. I fastened the seat belt across it.

"Well, hello, Matzo Ball," Nanu said, peering into the carrier.

"Thanks for letting the cat come too," Dad said as he got into the front passenger seat. "We hope you don't mind."

Matzo Ball leaned his forehead against the black bars so that Nanu could scratch it. She obliged.

"I don't mind," said Nanu. "But we'll have to wait and see what Moneypenny thinks!"

Then she got back into the golf cart, fastened her seat belt, and we were off.

Almost everyone on Marble Island drives a golf cart rather than a regular car. And everyone knows Nanu. People waved as we passed and called out, "Hi there, Agnes!" and "Hey, Ms. Wermer!"

Nanu waved and smiled like she was the queen of the island.

There aren't any traffic lights on Marble Island, and not that many stop signs. Mostly there are yellow triangle Yield signs, and people are so friendly that they take forever to decide who should stop and who should go, just waving each other through and saying things like "Ladies first!" and "You go on, I'm in no rush!" and "After you, I insist!"

It's totally different than what driving is like at home. There, people only seem to be happy if they're honking at each other, and everyone's always rushing, rushing, rushing.

"How is Moneypenny, Mom?" Dad asked Nanu.

"Oh, she's pretty good. A little crabby, but that's her right, isn't it?"

We drove down Main Street and under a big sign that read "Welcome to Marble Island. Stay for a While."

Usually I loved that sign. It meant that we were visiting Nanu for a few days, or maybe a week. But

this time, it felt different. I really would be staying for a while. Two whole months. I'd never been away from home without Mom and Dad for longer than a weekend.

I didn't want to think about that, so instead I concentrated on the wonderful scent of waffle cones baking at the ice cream shop. My mouth began to water.

"Nanu, can we stop for ice cream?"

"Sure," she said, but Dad said, "Maybe later, Harriet, you just had a doughnut."

"I only had one bite of the doughnut," I said. "It was stale."

"Harriet," Dad said in his deeper, I-know-that's-not-the-truth voice. But it was mostly true! I'd only had a few bites of the doughnut, and it had been sort of stale.

I was going to argue with him, but then Nanu said, "Let's get ice cream later. After we've gotten

Matzo Ball settled in."

That was a good idea, so I didn't complain. Nanu stuck her arm out the open side of the golf cart to indicate to other drivers that she was going to make a left turn onto Coral Reef Way, but then she recognized someone and her hand signal turned into a wave.

"Here we are," she said just a moment later, pulling the golf cart to a stop. "Home sweet home!"

There it was. The Bric-a-Brac B&B. Three stories tall, violet paint with purple trim, and a sunshiny-yellow front door. It was bright and cheerful and full of color, just like Nanu.

Big pots sat on each step leading up to the porch, flowers pouring out of them in a rainbow of colors, bees and butterflies meandering in lazy loops. On the far side of the porch was a ramp you could take if you wanted to avoid the stairs, and a row of flowerpots lined that too. On the porch were four big white wooden rocking chairs, two on each side of the door.

And there, poking up in the window on the right, were the droopy ears and disapproving glare of the one and only Moneypenny.

5

Harriet's Hideaway

"HISTORICALLY," NANU TOLD US AS we headed up the steps to the front door, "Moneypenny has not been a fan of cats."

She carried Matzo Ball's carrier, and I dragged Dadu's old suitcase. Boy, was it heavy! It was a good thing I didn't have to carry it very far.

"Moneypenny is more of a people person than a cat person," Nanu said, pushing open the tall yellow door.

I heard the clickety-clackety of Moneypenny's claws as she hopped down from the window seat and trotted slowly across the room to greet us. It must have been a pretty scary jump for a dog like Moneypenny, all the way down from the window seat to the floor. Moneypenny was a basset hound, which meant that her legs were only a few inches long, even though the rest of her was regular-dog-sized: a big barrel body, a long doggy snout, big brown mournful eyes, and—my favorite part—enormous, spatula-shaped ears, so long they brushed the floor.

"Moneypenny!" I said. I dropped the suitcase just inside the door—what a relief—and crouched down.

Moneypenny was glad to see me. I could tell because she came right over and shoved her big wet nose right against my neck and snorted warm wet breaths against me. I rubbed her big velvety ears.

I was glad to see her too. And even though I hadn't wanted to come, it was nice to be back at the Bric-a-Brac B&B. For one thing, the Bric-a-Brac B&B always smelled like cake frosting. That was something I'd forgotten until I smelled it again. And it was full of interesting trinkets and neat old furniture. And Moneypenny was always glad to see me.

But then I guess Moneypenny caught a whiff of cat smell, and Matzo Ball caught a whiff of dog smell. And the two of them seemed to agree on one thing—that our coming to the island was a terrible idea.

From inside his carrier, Matzo Ball growled, his orangey fur puffing up to make him really look like a big angry ball.

Suddenly, Moneypenny realized that there was a cat in her house. She growled back, and then she barked—really loud!

Bark! Bark bark!

"Moneypenny," said Nanu. "You know the rules about barking in the house."

Moneypenny *did* seem to know the rules, because she stopped barking. She didn't stop sniffing at Matzo Ball through the carrier, though. I guess there was no rule about sniffing.

"Come on, Harriet, let's take Matzo Ball and your luggage upstairs," Nanu said.

I think when Moneypenny heard the word "upstairs," she lost interest in following us. I don't blame her! If my legs were three inches long, I wouldn't want to go up or down stairs any more often than absolutely necessary.

And there were *a lot* of stairs. The main floor of the Bric-a-Brac B&B had the kitchen and the dining area and one guest room and a big sitting room full of squishy chairs and tables full of books and a tall dollhouse and a fireplace and a cabinet with games and puzzles.

The second story had the rest of the guest rooms, each door labeled with a little wooden sign—the Captain's Cove and the Lovebirds' Lookout and the Romantic Retreat—blech! You never knew who you might run into at Nanu's B and B, but so far we hadn't seen anyone other than Nanu and Moneypenny, which was just fine by me. I wasn't in the mood to meet anyone.

Then there was another staircase, this one steeper and skinnier, that led to the third floor, and Nanu's apartment. No guests came up here, and this was where we stayed when we visited. I was huffing and puffing by the time we got there, and I set down Dadu's old suitcase with a loud thump. I was definitely regretting having packed my rock collection. Nanu, though, was barely breathing hard at all! I guess she was used to all the steps. And then up came Dad, looking a little gray in the face from carrying up the big suitcase and the duffel bag at the same time.

"Walter, you could have taken two trips," Nanu said.

"You know I don't believe in taking two trips," said Dad, but it took him about five breaths to get out all those words.

"Let's set up Matzo Ball in your room," Nanu said.

I followed Nanu down the short hallway. Her room was at the end, near the bathroom. There was another small bedroom on the left, and that was where we went.

"I'll put a litterbox in the bathroom for Matzo Ball," said Nanu, "and I think the two of you should be snug as a couple of bugs in here." She handed me Matzo Ball's carrier.

There was a little wooden sign on the door that hadn't been there last time we visited. It read "Harriet's Hideaway."

"Aww, Mom, that's a nice touch," Dad said.

And it really was. It was nice that Nanu was trying to make this feel special for me. But seeing that sign on the door reminded me that I wasn't just visiting for the weekend. I was going to spend the whole summer here.

Sometimes, I can tell I'm either going to get really sad or I'm going to get really mad. And mad feels better than sad.

"Hideaway is a dumb word," I said. And then I went into the room and slammed closed the door—hard—leaving Dad and Nanu outside.

6

Don't Cry

DAD COULDN'T EVEN STAY TO have lunch with us, but I don't want to talk about that.

He had to race right back to the dock so that he could take the very next ferryboat home. Because Mom was on bed rest, and she couldn't be left alone for very long. He'd left her lots of snacks by the bed, but he needed to get back to make her lunch.

He told me all this through the slammed-closed door to my new room. Actually, almost as soon as I'd slammed it, I was sorry. But you can't *unslam* a door. And on the inside of it, all alone, I knew I was wasting the little bit of Dad time I had left.

"Harriet?" Dad said, after he was all through telling me about how he had to leave and asking if I wanted to come say goodbye. Then he knocked on the door, like we didn't even live together anymore.

I pulled it open and said, "I didn't slam it. A burst of wind must have blown it closed."

Maybe Dad believed me. Anyway, he didn't say anything. He just reached out and hugged me.

I wanted him to hug me. I liked the smell of his shirt and the strong feel of his arms and the way he was warm and tall. But I also *didn't* want him to hug me because I was mad. I counted to three in my head and then pushed him away, even though I didn't want to.

"I'm going to come visit you the weekend after next," Dad said.

"I don't care," I said. But in my head I was saying Don't cry don't cry don't cry.

Dad sniffed and rubbed his hand across his eyes. "I'm going to miss you a million zillion, Harriet," he said, and he pulled me into another hug and kissed the top of my head.

I took another big, deep breath of the smell of him, and I squeezed my eyes shut tight. "That's not even a real number," I said. My voice sounded weird all squished up against his stomach.

Pretty soon after that, Dad went downstairs. Nanu went with him. I went back into my room and watched out the window, looking down at the front porch and waiting for Dad to come outside.

"Meow," said Matzo Ball.

"Oh! Sorry, buddy," I said, and I unzipped his kitty carrier. He stuck his fluffy head out of the carrier and sniffed the air, then stepped halfway out.

Matzo Ball always tries to be brave, but really he's a scaredy-cat.

I scratched his head real quick, but then I went back to the window. Still no Dad. I started to worry that maybe he'd already come out of the Bric-a-Brac B&B and was on his way to the dock and I'd missed seeing him. But that's when the front door swung open, and then I could see the top of his head. He was holding his baseball cap in his hand. I'd never really seen the top of Dad's head this clearly. On the tippy-top, in the middle of his dark-brown hair, I saw a little patch of skin.

"Hey!" I called down.

Dad looked up. He had a big wide smile. "There's my girl!" he said.

"Did you know you have a bald spot on the top of your head?"

I was sort of sorry I said it almost as soon as the words came out. Sometimes I say things and I don't know why I say them.

But Dad didn't seem mad. He grinned up at me and waved, a big wide friendly wave. "Love you, Harriet," he said.

"Love you, Dad," I answered, and then I watched him put his hat back on and walk up the street toward the ferry.

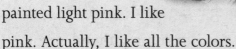

Then I flopped down on the bed and stared up at the ceiling. It was painted light pink. I like pink. Actually, I like all the colors.

Even though Dad was gone, I was starting to feel a little better. It was like when you have a splinter and then finally it gets yanked out—your finger is still a little sore, but it's better than before.

Matzo Ball seemed to agree with me. He jumped up onto the bed and bumped my forehead with his forehead.

"Meow," he said.

"Meow," I said back to him.

I sat up. The rest of the room was just as nice as the ceiling; all the furniture was made of dark-brown wood, and the bed was way bigger than my bed at home, and Nanu liked to put lots of pillows *everywhere*. Pillows and books. There was a stack of interesting-looking books on the table next to the bed, with a big white shell on top.

I picked up the shell. Its white outside was sort of dull and rough, but the inside part was smooth and shiny. It felt good to rub my thumb across it. Rough then smooth then rough.

I went to the closet and pulled open the door. It was pretty much empty except for a pair of over-alls on a hanger. They were dark blue denim, and they were dotted with little faded patches of paint here and there. They looked just about exactly my size. I pulled them off the hanger and kicked off my shoes.

They fit perfectly, except the left shoulder strap felt a little tight. I shoved my hands into the deep pockets. They were the most comfortable thing I'd ever worn. I decided right then that I'd wear them all summer, and making that decision felt good. Like I still had some control over some things, even if I didn't have control over lots of other things.

"Want to go see the rest of the place, Matzo Ball?" I asked.

He didn't. He'd found a pillow to sit on and was busy tucking his feet into kitten position.

Nanu wasn't anywhere in the little third floor apartment—not in the main room, not in the little kitchen, not in her bedroom. The bathroom door was swung wide open, and she wasn't in there, either.

So I went downstairs, all the way to the ground floor. I found Nanu in the sitting room, the one with the fireplace and all the flyers about Marble Island activities and the games and puzzles and stuff. She was sitting in a chair by the front window, reading a book. Next to her, on the window seat, was Moneypenny, keeping an eye on the front yard. There was a little staircase with just three stairs pushed up against the window seat. Moneypenny could jump down, but she was way too long and low to get up there on her own.

Nanu looked up from her book and smiled at me. "They *do* fit," she said. "I thought they would."

I felt sort of shy. "Thanks for the overalls."

She stood up and adjusted the left shoulder strap. Now it felt perfect. "I've been waiting for you to get big enough to fit into these," she said. "They were your dad's, you know, when he was about your age."

"Really?"

"He wore them for years, until he couldn't fasten the straps anymore."

"Do you have any more of his stuff? Like, in the basement, or anything?"

Nanu shook her head. "The B and B doesn't have a basement. And your dad gave away most of his kid stuff when he went away to college, the rest when he and your mom got married. I kept the overalls because they were so . . . Well, they reminded me so much of your dad, I just couldn't let them go. Now they're yours."

I thought I remembered Dad saying that he used to hang out in the basement of Nanu's house, but I guess I was wrong. I felt like arguing, but it didn't make much sense to argue about a basement. I don't know why, but all of a sudden I felt this big hot bubble in my chest and my nose got all stuffy and my eyes started to burn.

"It's okay to cry, Harriet," Nanu said. "This is a big change."

I didn't want to cry. I balled up my hands and shoved them into my pockets. Then I thought about how when my dad was a kid, he must have shoved his hands into these same pockets, and then I felt tears sliding down my cheeks.

Nanu hugged me, and I let her. She was shorter and softer than Dad. "You know," she said, and I felt her warm breath on my head, "your dad had lots of adventures on the island in those overalls. Maybe you can have some this summer too."

"I've already done all the island stuff, Nanu."

"Well," she said, and she kissed my head, then tilted up my chin to look me in the eyes, "adventure and mystery are everywhere, if you know how to look." She turned to Moneypenny. Something had gotten her excited; she sniffed the window-pane and licked it with her long, pink tongue.

"It's probably just a fly or something."

"Maybe," said Nanu. "Maybe not. Want to take Moneypenny out front to investigate?"

7

Tip Troller

MONEYPENNY WAS SO EXCITED TO get in her harness to go outside that she started to drool. *A lot.*

"Is she okay?" I asked Nanu. My right arm looked like the world's biggest snail had crawled across it. Sticky and drippy and gross.

"She's just perfect," Nanu said, looking at Moneypenny like it was gold coming out of her mouth rather than drool.

"Come on, Moneypenny." I finally got the

harness fastened around her chest. She trotted toward the door.

I didn't want to wipe my drooly arm on my new overalls, so as soon as we got onto the front porch, I ran my arm along the wooden railing. Blech.

"Have fun, girls!" Nanu waved at us from the door.

Moneypenny panted, tired already from the excitement of putting on the harness and stepping onto the porch. When she started to go down the stairs, she reminded me of a slinky—all long and wobbly. Her legs were so short that I started to worry that she might flip over like a slinky, too, but she managed to make it down to the sidewalk.

Then she stood panting, and looked up at me like she was asking, "Now what?"

"Beats me," I told her. "You were the one who was so excited to come outside."

Finally Moneypenny decided to go left, up the

block and away from the shore. Even though I'd
been visiting the island all of my life, I didn't really
know any of the neighbors here. When we visited,
we were usually hanging around the B and B, or

out doing all the fun tourist stuff, like snorkeling and riding around in glass-bottom boats and feeding the garibaldi, which are these big orange fish who will eat right out of your hand, like housecats.

This time, as we walked slowly up the block, I looked at each house and wondered who lived inside. Lots of the houses were vacation rentals. They had signs out front with the name of the company you could call if you wanted to stay there. But a few of the houses looked more like regular places where people actually lived. These houses were a little less neat, with messy front porches and mismatched chairs and front doors that needed a coat of paint.

A golf cart wheeled by with an electric hum, and the driver honked merrily. "Hi, Moneypenny!" called the family inside, waving furiously as if Moneypenny were some sort of celebrity.

She ignored the attention and just shuffled along, sniffing the sidewalk as she went.

Three houses up, she squatted to pee, and then she was ready to head back. Luckily, I didn't need to use the little bag Nanu had made me bring along. I shoved it into the back pocket of my overalls.

Just like I'd thought, there was no great exciting adventure out here. Moneypenny had only wanted to go to the bathroom. It doesn't get more boring than that.

At the base of the B and B's staircase, Moneypenny stopped and looked mournfully up.

"You can do it, Moneypenny," I said, but I wasn't totally sure she could. So I led her over to the ramp instead. Her ears were so long that they swept a path on both sides of her body.

Some people were clambering up the steps from the street right as Moneypenny and I reached the porch. They looked youngish and they smiled brightly, and they were both carrying luggage.

I don't know why, but their smiles made me mad.

"Hello," said the woman. She was wearing a white T-shirt that said "Mrs. Martin" in fancy cursive. "Are you staying here too?"

"No," I said. "I'm just the dog walker." I don't know why I lied.

"Would you mind getting the door?" asked the man. He was wearing a T-shirt that read "Mr. Martin" in the same fancy handwriting. They must have just gotten married.

"I would," I said, "but there's something wrong with my thumbs."

"Oh," said Mrs. Martin. She looked concerned, and she set down her suitcase. "Did you fall down?"

"It's okay," I said. "I'll be all right in a minute."

She pulled open the door and waited for me to go in first.

Moneypenny led the way, picking up a trot for the first time. She made a beeline for the parlor and flopped into a shady corner on the cool hardwood floor. I undid her harness and untangled her from the leash, doing my best to ignore the newlyweds.

"Welcome to the Bric-a-Brac B&B," said Nanu. "I see you've met Moneypenny and my granddaughter already."

I could feel the newlyweds staring at me, but I didn't look back at them. I sort of cringed and waited for them to tell Nanu I'd lied to them about just being the dog walker.

But all Mr. Martin said was, "We sure did!" and all Mrs. Martin said was, "What a beautiful place!"

Nanu went over to the desk and did all the checking-in stuff, and then she said, "Harriet, why don't you show these nice people to the Romantic Retreat. Mr. and Mrs. Martin, if you need anything at all, just ask. Wine and cheese in the parlor at five p.m., breakfast tomorrow morning at nine o'clock."

I couldn't think of a good way to get out of it,

so I said, "Right this way," and I started to walk to the staircase.

"Help them with their bags, Harriet," called Nanu, but Mr. Martin said, "That's all right, we've got it. We wouldn't want her to hurt her thumbs."

"Her thumbs?" Nanu asked.

"Welcome to the Bric-a-Brac B&B," I said loudly, waving my hand toward the staircase. "Right this way to the Romantic Retreat." And then I took the stairs double-time before there could be any more conversation about my thumbs.

When we got to the second floor, I led the way to the door marked "Romantic Retreat."

"Here you go," I said. And then, because they could have told Nanu about my lie but didn't, I added, "I hope you have a nice visit."

"Thank you very much," Mr. Martin said, and he reached into his wallet and pulled out a five-dollar bill, then handed it to me.

"What's this for?" I asked.

"It's a tip. For bringing us up to our room."

Slowly, I folded the bill and tucked it into my pocket. Hmm. A tip.

"If you need anything else," I said, "like towels or a bucket of ice, just let me know."

"We would," said Mrs. Martin with a smile, "but we wouldn't want you to strain your thumbs."

"Oh, those," I said, bending my thumbs to show they were working fine. "Don't worry about my thumbs. They're feeling much better."

"That's a relief," said Mrs. Martin. "All right then, we'll let you know if we need anything. Nice to meet you, Harriet." Then they went into the Romantic Retreat.

I stood in the hallway, thinking. Five dollars, just for walking up some stairs! I didn't even carry their luggage.

So I went to the door that read "Captain's Cove" and knocked.

"Coming, coming," said a deep woman's voice. I heard the squeak of a chair being pushed back, and then slow heavy footsteps crossing the room.

The door opened. I looked up . . . and up . . . and up. The woman was so tall that her head almost touched the doorframe. And she was wide, too, built like a refrigerator. Her head was covered by bushy dark-gray hair, the color of metal.

"Can I help you?" she asked.

I cleared my throat. "Actually," I said, "I was wondering if I could help you. I'm Harriet. If you need anything—like, ice, maybe?—I can bring it to your room."

"Ah," said the woman. "A tip troller, are you?"

I didn't know exactly what she meant by that, but it didn't sound good. I just shrugged.

"Thank you, Harriet. I'm fine for now." As she closed her door, I caught sight of the desk behind her, underneath the window. It was covered with papers and open books, and a laptop. It didn't look like the desk of a person on vacation.

I wanted to ask her about it, but then the door was shut, and I heard Nanu's voice from downstairs. "Harriet. What are you doing?"

Rats. I'd have to knock on the last door some other time.

"Nothing," I lied, and then I went downstairs.

Nanu was there, at the bottom of the staircase, looking up at me like maybe she suspected I wasn't telling her the whole story. Then she said, "Harriet, I can tell you're the kind of person who needs a job. Isn't that right?"

"No," I said. "It isn't. I'm the kind of person who needs ice cream."

Nanu smiled. "That's right," she said. "I promised ice cream. And we'll get some. But first, how about you work up an appetite?"

8

Nanu's Shed

NANU LED ME THROUGH THE front room and into the dining room. She went over to the big wood-and-glass cabinet that was built into the far corner. She opened the bottom set of drawers and pulled out a big, rectangular wooden box. It looked heavy.

"This is something very special," she said. "Something I wouldn't trust just anyone with."

She set the box down on the dining table and

gestured to me to open it. I had to admit, I felt a little bit excited.

As I cracked open the box, I could see the inside was lined with green velvet. It looked expensive. And sure enough, it was full of—

Silverware. Boring old forks and spoons and knives. Not even *sharp* knives! The dull kind, for spreading butter.

I looked over at Nanu. Was she joking or something? She didn't look like she was joking. She looked down at the boring old silverware practically the same way she looked at Moneypenny.

"This silverware belonged to my grandmother. One day, Harriet, it will belong to you. But right now, it needs a good polishing. What do you say? Are you the right girl for the job?"

Well, I didn't even know what to say to that. I love Nanu, and I didn't want to hurt her feelings . . . but *silverware?*

I closed the box. I didn't *mean* to slam it. Then I said, "Nanu, I have a better idea for a summer job."

I led her down the hallway next to the kitchen to the back door. She followed me across the back garden full of flowers and little seating areas and funny little paths and plants and one big tree—all the way to the very farthest part of the yard. The whole back wall was covered over with a plant Nanu called creeping fig, and you couldn't even tell what the wall was made out of—wood or stone or brick. It looked like it was just made out of waxy green leaves and vines.

The creeping fig was doing its job, creeping all along the wall and even creeping up the side of Nanu's shed, which looked like a miniature house. It had two little windows that were covered over with closed shutters and it had a flower box beneath each one. It had a pointy roof with scalloped roof tiles and a skinny wooden door that was painted yellow to match the door of the Bric-a-Brac B&B. If it wasn't so stuffed with ancient junk, Nanu's shed would make a pretty good playhouse.

But I wasn't interested in playhouses then. I was thinking about what Dad had said on the ferry. That he had always wondered if something good might be hidden in there. I couldn't help but sort of wonder too.

I turned the rusty doorknob and pushed open the creaky door. The shed smelled like dust and old stuff. Nanu sneezed and I blinked, trying to see into the darkness.

"Instead of polishing silverware, Nanu," I said, "how about if I clean out the shed?"

"Hmm," said Nanu doubtfully.

I was starting to be able to see shapes and shadows in the darkness: a big hulking thing way in the back, slumped over like a sleeping giant; odd-shaped objects filling three long shelves on the left side of the shed; boxes and trunks and baskets stacked all catawampus on the other side.

"Well . . . I never have been able to make heads or tails of this whole mess," Nanu finally said. "The truth is, I don't even know what all is in there anymore."

Nanu's arm waved around in the air in the middle of the shed, like she was sweeping away cobwebs. I hadn't considered *spiders*.

Actually, staring at the mess, I was beginning to feel doubtful too. Like the time Dad had taken a roast chicken out of the oven and was letting it "rest"—I don't know why a *cooked chicken* would need to *rest*— and Matzo Ball pulled the whole chicken off the counter onto the floor, and when we'd all run into the kitchen, he was looking all worried like he was thinking, "This is bigger than I thought it would be." That was the way I was feeling now, peering into the dusty, crowded shed. Like I'd bitten off more than I could chew.

I shivered and started to back out of the shed, but then Nanu found what she was looking for—a string that she pulled, turning on a bare light bulb that hung from the ceiling.

With the light bulb on, the shed looked less spooky and more like a regular mess.

"You know," said Nanu, "The shutters actually open, and there are real glass windowpanes behind all this." She waved at the walls, stacked tall with bowls and dishes and platters and things. The boxes on the other end were mostly cardboard, a few wooden crates mixed in. Anything could be in them. The big giant-shaped thing was probably a piece of furniture, covered with an old tarp splashed with paint of all different colors. I guessed it was just an old chest of drawers, but who could say?

I was starting to feel excited again.

"I can sort it out," I said. I wasn't sure if that was the truth or a lie. "I'll separate out the broken stuff from the good stuff and organize it into piles."

"Well then," Nanu said, "I'll leave you to it. Try not to make a great big mess in the main part of the yard. The guests like to sit out there in the evenings. And if you find anything really special, or if you need help with anything heavy, you just give me a holler."

Then Nanu headed back to the B and B, leaving the shed door wide open.

That was a good thing about Nanu. She wasn't one of those grown-ups who thought that just because a person was a kid, that meant they couldn't do things, like cleaning out a shed or being trusted not to mess stuff up. I liked that about her.

"Well then," I said, just like Nanu had, only I wasn't talking to anybody but myself. "Let's see what the giant really is, first thing."

I went over and grabbed the tarp with both hands. In my mind, I imagined myself yanking it off in one fell swoop, revealing whatever was underneath all dramatically. But in real life, the tarp got snagged on something. I had to scooch a bunch of boxes out of the way so I could fit behind the thing and figure out what the problem was. Then, a whole cloud of dust came off the boxes, and I had to stop and sneeze for a while until it settled down.

Finally I found the problem—the tarp was stuck on a nail that was sticking out a little ways from the back of whatever the thing was—and then, at last, I got the darned thing off.

And there it was . . . exactly what I'd guessed it would be. An old dresser, three drawers high and two drawers wide, all scratched up and ugly. Two of the drawer handles were broken, and one was missing altogether.

That made me feel like giving up. It was silly to think that there could be something cool out here in this old shed, but I guess some part of me had hoped to find a real treasure under that old dirty tarp.

Still, I had a job to do, and I decided that the best way to clean up the shed would be to move the chest outside to make a little room. It would be lighter without the drawers, so I started pulling them out one by one and taking them out of the shed.

It wasn't until I took out the third drawer that I found it.

I had put the third drawer on top of the other two, and was turning back to go get the fourth, when the sparkle of something caught my eye, way in the very back of the drawer, half hidden by the old flower-print paper lining the bottom.

I grabbed it and pulled it out. It was heavy, made of old metal, turning green from age. The top end was shaped like a three-leaf clover with pointy shapes in the middle that looked like mountains, and the bottom was like mismatched teeth, all different lengths. I held up the key to look at the mountain shapes more closely. Four interconnected peaks.

It didn't look much like any of the keys I'd ever seen in real life, but that's what it was. A really, really old key.

"If there's a key," I said out loud, but really quiet, in case anyone was listening, "there must be a lock that it opens."

Nanu had said that if I found anything special, I should give her a holler. This key seemed pretty special to me. But rather than calling for Nanu, before anyone could see what I'd found, I slipped the key into the top pocket of my overalls. I patted my pocket and felt the shape of the key, and the fast beating of my heart too.

I was excited the same way Matzo Ball was whenever he saw a lizard in the yard. Like something great was about to happen, if only he could figure out how to catch it.

9

Hans & Gretchen's Ice Cream Parlor

FINDING THAT KEY MADE ME feel all nervous and excited. I definitely didn't feel like doing any more work in the shed. I patted the pocket with the hidden key again, and then I went back inside.

Nanu was half disappeared into the refrigerator, digging way in the back.

"Nanu?" I asked. "What are you doing?"

She pulled out her head. Her hair was wild. "I thought I had more olallieberry jam," she said, "but it seems like I'm fresh out. We can pick some up on our way to the ice cream shop. You ready to go?"

I was.

Nanu put on her yellow hat and picked up her shoulder bag. She hung a little sign on the door that read "Back in a Jiffy!" and then asked Moneypenny if she wanted to come with us.

Moneypenny, who was half asleep on the window seat, a ray of sunshine across her long body, didn't reply. So we left her there and out we went.

We walked up the street toward the beach and the shops. I'd walked up this street lots of times, but never with a hidden key in my pocket. Suddenly, all I could see was keyholes: doors on houses and padlocks on bicycles and ignitions of golf carts parked along the curbs. I knew the key in my pocket didn't belong to any of these keyholes, but still, my fingers itched to pull out the key and look at it more closely. And I was wondering about the thing Dad had mentioned, the house with treasure inside. What had he called it? Treasure was usually locked away in something. Something that needs a key.

I went with Nanu into the corner market. She went straight to the jam aisle and found two jars of olallieberry. "This is the best jam for fresh scones," she said, either to me or the cashier or both of us. She tucked the jam jars into her shoulder bag and then we went on our way to the ice cream shop.

I followed the smell of fresh waffle cones. Even if I hadn't been to the ice cream shop tons of times, I'll bet I could have found my way just by the smell.

There it was: Hans & Gretchen's Ice Cream Parlor.

It had a green Dutch door—that's a door that is cut in half so you can open the top and not the bottom—and a little thatched roof and window boxes full of flowers. Gretchen's job was to make the ice cream, and Hans's job was to sell it. Nanu said they'd been making and selling ice cream on Marble Island for fifty years. She said they'd come there on their honeymoon and never left.

For the first time, I took a good look at the lock on the green Dutch door. I'd never noticed it before. Now, I saw that it had a tall, skinny keyhole. The key in my pocket was about that tall, but wider. Not that I expected the key to open the door to Hans & Gretchen's Ice Cream Parlor, but looking at the old green door made me think—I'd bet my key proba- bly opened something old and big.

"Harriet!" called Hans as soon as we pushed through the Dutch door. He stood right where he always stood, behind the counter. And just like always, he wore an apron the same shade of green as the Dutch door. Hans liked to say that he was as Dutch as the door. Hans didn't look anything like the door—he had sun-chapped reddish skin and a thick white mustache that went all the way up the sides of his face. Nanu had told me that style was called "muttonchops."

"Look at you!" Hans said. "Tall as a sunflower, you're getting. And you're looking more like your father every day."

It was hard to be crabby in an ice cream shop. "Hi, Hans. It's nice to see you again."

"Gretchen!" Hans called into the kitchen. "Come see what the tide washed up!"

Gretchen pushed through the swinging kitchen doors, wiping her hands on her apron. Hans was tall and thin and Gretchen was short and round, like he was a cone and she was a scoop of ice cream. And she wore her white hair way up on top of her head, like whipped cream on a sundae. "Why, hello, Harriet! Agnes, you didn't tell us your grandgirl was coming for a visit. Is Walter here too?"

Then Nanu told them all the stuff about Mom

and the baby and bed rest and how I'd be there all summer and how I'd even brought my cat, but I didn't want to hear it. I'd finally stopped thinking about all that stuff and here they were bringing it all up again!

So I said loudly, "I'll have a double scoop of vanilla on a waffle cone, please."

Technically I *was* interrupting, but I *did* say "please," so I guess I was sort of hoping that would even things out.

But the grown-ups totally ignored me until they were done talking, which is just as rude as inter-rupting, maybe even ruder, if you want my opinion.

When they were done, Hans turned to me and said, "So, Harriet, what can I get for you today?" even though I *know* he definitely heard what I said the first time.

"I'll have a double scoop of vanilla on a waffle cone," I repeated. This time I left off the "please."

Rather than scooping my ice cream, Hans stood there with his arms folded, like he was waiting for something.

"Please," I added, but I wasn't happy about it.

Then he said, "Vanilla again, Harriet? Don't you want to try something new? Maybe pistachio? Or licorice? I have some in the back, just made. It's one of the new flavors we're thinking of debuting at the Centennial."

I wouldn't have asked for vanilla ice cream if I wanted pistachio ice cream or licorice ice cream. But I didn't say this. I just folded my arms like Hans had done, and after a minute he laughed and shook his head, and scooped my vanilla.

"How is the party planning coming along?" Nanu asked, and they talked for a few minutes about something I didn't care about, so I licked my cone and ignored them until they were done.

There were a bunch of plaques on the wall. Each one had a picture of the winner along with

information about what they'd won for. I liked to look at them every time I came into the ice cream shop. All of them were for winners of various ice cream contests:

FASTEST BANANA SPLIT EATER

TALLEST ICE-CREAM CONE—SEVEN SCOOPS

LONGEST STREAK—211 DAYS IN A ROW

That last one had a picture of my dad back when he was a teenager. His hair was big and curly and wild. He was smiling and holding a double scoop of vanilla, just like me. Sometimes I forgot that my dad used to be a kid, and that he grew up here on Marble Island.

Finally, Nanu asked for a scoop of strawberry ice cream in a cup, and we said goodbye. Before we left, Hans said, "Say hello to your dad for us, will you? And tell him next time he's on the island, he'd better stop by for a scoop and a hug. You know, Harriet, your dad used to come in here wearing a pair of overalls that looked just like those. He loved wandering around the village and visiting all the shops and getting to know all the neighbors. He was a curious fellow, your father."

"Curious how?"

"In both senses of the word, actually! Curious means full of questions, which your father certainly was. But it also means . . . unusual. Your father was both. He always had interesting things in his pockets—little paintbrushes and tiny screwdrivers and itty-bitty nails."

That didn't sound like my dad. As Nanu and I ate our ice cream and walked back to the Bric-a-Brac B&B, I tried to imagine my dad as a kid, walking up this same sidewalk, even licking the same sort of ice cream. I wondered if the stuff he used to carry around—the little paintbrushes and the tiny screwdrivers and the itty-bitty nails—could have anything to do with the treasure he'd mentioned on the ferry. And I thought about the key I'd found, tucked into the front pocket of my overalls, and the stuff my dad used to put in these same pockets when he was a kid, including his hands.

Thinking about my dad's hands reminded me of how he'd put his big, warm hand on my shoulder when we were on the ferry. That was only a little while ago. And now Dad was on the ferry again, crossing the ocean toward home, getting farther and farther away from me. Maybe the ferry had already docked and he was in the car driving home. I didn't want to think about that.

But even though I didn't want to talk about Dad or think about him, I said, "I'll bet Matzo Ball will be glad to have a nice long break from my dad. Do you know what Dad did yesterday? He rolled Matzo Ball right off a pillow, when he was fast asleep! Can you believe that?"

Nanu ate another spoonful of her strawberry ice cream. Then she said, "You're going to really miss your parents. And I know they will really miss you too. I'll bet they are missing you already."

Stupid tears. Stupid missing. I shook my head. "No," I said. "As long as I have Matzo Ball, I am just fine."

10

Bubble Machine

THE WORST TIME TO HAVE a bad dream is when you're spending the night somewhere that isn't your own house with your own bed.

Nightmares are bad enough when you're safe and sound in the room you've slept in most of your life, but when you're having one in a bed you're not used to, they're a hundred times worse.

The bad dream I had the first night at the Bric-a-Brac B&B was about falling down stairs. Maybe it was because of all the stairs at the B and B. In my dream the stairs got steeper and steeper and then they turned into a ramp and I was falling falling falling and then whomp!

I woke up on the floor in a tangle of sheets and blankets and I didn't know which way was up or even where I was.

My heart was pounding and my face was wet with tears. Then—this is the worst part—I realized that other parts of me were wet too. I felt mad and embarrassed.

The curtains were halfway open and light from the moon made the room just shadowy instead of totally dark. Matzo Ball looked down at me from his place on my pillow. He blinked at me but didn't move to help.

"Thanks a lot, Matzo Ball," I said. Then I got up and untangled myself from the sheets. Luckily I'd fallen out of the bed before I'd had my accident, so the mattress wasn't wet. After I changed into clean jammies, I balled up all the sheets and my wet clothes and snuck out of my room. The rest of the top floor apartment was quiet. I hadn't woken up Nanu or Moneypenny.

Where did Nanu keep her washing machine? I couldn't find it, and then I realized it must be on the bottom floor somewhere, which was probably a good thing since if I started a washing machine up here in the middle of the night, I'd definitely wake everyone up.

So then I had to go down all those stairs, carrying my big awkward dumb bundle of sheets. It made me so mad, the whole thing. Mad at myself, mad at my dad for sending me to this dumb island, mad at Nanu for letting me have a second glass of apple juice before bed.

Mad at all these stairs.

I tiptoed through the second floor, past all the

closed guest room doors. The hall was totally dark except for a thin strip of light beneath the door to the Captain's Cove. What was she doing awake this late? I walked extra carefully past her door.

Finally I was on the bottom floor and I let out all the breath I'd been holding. The laundry machine was on the far side of the kitchen. It was a funny-looking laundry machine. At home, our machine opened on the top, but this one had a window door on the front. I shoved all the sheets and my jammies inside, but then I couldn't find laundry soap anywhere. There was some blue liquid soap under the kitchen sink, so I squirted a bunch of that inside instead and started the darn machine.

I headed toward the staircase, but something caught my eye in the front room. It was Nanu's dollhouse, on a table in the corner. It had been there all my life. When I was little, I used to like helping Nanu switch out the summer decorations for winter decorations. I hadn't really looked at it in years. But right then, Nanu's dollhouse looked just like a—

Gingerbread house.

That was what Dad had mentioned on the ferry. *That's where the real treasure is,* he'd said.

I wanted to turn on all the lights in the B and B and check out the dollhouse right then. But it was too late, and I'd made enough of a mess as it was. I'd take a closer look tomorrow.

Upstairs, Matzo Ball had fallen back asleep and he was taking up the whole pillow. I lay down on the bare mattress and pulled the blanket up over my shoulders. I wasn't very comfortable without a pillow, but I wasn't about to make Matzo Ball move. And when I fell back to sleep, I didn't have any more dreams.

There are some sounds that you can sleep right through. But there are some sounds that wake you up, no matter how soundly you are sleeping.

Nanu's laugh is one of those sounds.

It woke up Matzo Ball too! He yawned and stuck out his scratchy pink tongue.

Together, we followed the sound of Nanu's laughter—as big and loud and yellow as her hat—all the way down to the first floor, through the great big sitting room, into the kitchen, and then . . .

Nanu and Moneypenny were wading through a sea of bubbles. Moneypenny was practically swimming! The bubbles came up to her chest.

Cats don't like water and they don't like bubbles. Matzo Ball took one sniff and turned right around.

"I didn't do it," I said. I didn't even mean to say anything, but the lie came out all on its own.

Nanu tried not to laugh, probably because she had remembered that there might still be sleeping guests, but I guess she thought the whole thing was so funny that she couldn't help herself, even though she put her hand over her mouth. Now her

laugh was making me mad. It sounded like she was laughing at *me*.

"I didn't do it," I said again, louder this time, and I stamped my foot in the bubbles. Moneypenny looked at me with her big mournful eyes. Bubbles dripped from her chin like a beard.

"All right, Harriet," Nanu said. She finally had her laughter under control and she wiped her eyes with a handkerchief that she pulled from a pocket. "I think between you, me, and Moneypenny, we can clear out these bubbles and still have time to get breakfast on the table for our guests. What do you say?"

What could I say? "Okay."

Nanu got the mop and I got the broom and Moneypenny got out of the way. We opened up the back door and swept and mopped and swept and mopped.

Then Nanu pulled my sheets and jammies out of the washer and rinsed them in the kitchen sink. She didn't even say anything about the fact that it was my stuff in there. She wiped the leftover bubbles out of the machine and put the laundry back inside.

"Here's where we keep the laundry soap," she said, opening the same cabinet I had looked in last night. But then she pulled down a pink tin box and took off the lid. It was filled with squishy little pods that looked like they could be sea animals of some kind. "Use two of these for a regular load, three for a large load."

I didn't say anything. I just nodded.

She started the machine again and then turned to me with a smile. "How do you feel about chocolate chip muffins?"

Was Nanu really not going to be mad at me? "I feel really good about chocolate chip muffins," I said. "Actually, I feel great about them."

"Okay," Nanu said, handing me an apron. "Then wash up! We've got work to do."

11

A Keyhole, a Key

BY NINE O'CLOCK, THE WHOLE downstairs was full. First came the woman who'd been awake in the middle of the night, the one who had called me a tip troller—I hadn't decided yet whether or not to forgive her. She drank her coffee black.

"Good morning, Captain," Nanu greeted her cheerily.

Then came the guests I hadn't met yet, the ones staying in Lovebirds' Lookout. It was a man and his son. The little kid told me they were celebrating his sixth birthday with a fishing trip to Marble Island. He also told me that yesterday they'd caught three fish but had to throw them all back because they were too small. He told me that his favorite part of the trip so far was the boat ride over. He told me that he didn't like wearing sunscreen but his dad made him. He told me that his name was Mateo and his dad's was too. And I'll bet he would have kept on telling me things all day if I hadn't practically shoved a chocolate chip muffin in his mouth. Then he got busy chewing.

The newlyweds came down last. "Good morning, Mrs. Martin! Good morning, Mr. Martin!" Nanu said, making a big deal of calling them "Mrs." and "Mr." because it was still so new for them. I thought it was pretty goofy, but they seemed to enjoy it. They barely stopped holding hands long enough to get themselves coffee (with lots of cream and sugar), but then they were right back at it, as if their hands were made of magnets.

"Good morning, Mrs. Wermer," they said, but Nanu said, "Oh, just call me Agnes."

Suddenly I realized something. My hand flew to the pocket on my overalls where the key was hidden, but then I dropped my hand down fast like it had touched a hot coal. No one seemed to notice, except for the woman Nanu had called "Captain," who I was beginning to think was the sort of person who noticed *everything*.

What had gotten me so excited was hearing the newlyweds call Nanu "Mrs. Wermer." Because it made me remember the four mountain peaks on the key. Maybe I had been holding the key upside down. Maybe they weren't mountains . . . they were *letters*. Two *W*s.

Nanu's last name is Wermer, just like ours. Her first name doesn't start with a *W* . . . but my dad's does. His name is Walter. That must be what the *W*s stood for: Walter Wermer.

Maybe the key was my dad's.

Pretty soon everyone got busy eating muffins and some people had eggs and me and Mateo (the little one) had hot chocolate. In my head I kept thinking *Walter Wermer, Walter Wermer, Walter Wermer*. My fingers were itching to reach into my pocket and pull out the key, to see if the shapes really were *W*s. I ate two muffins and had a second cup of hot chocolate just to keep my hands busy, and then I wandered over to the dollhouse to inspect it.

Now, in the light of the morning, it didn't look as much like a regular gingerbread house. But it *did* look mysterious. I could see now that it was almost a miniature version of the B and B. The outside was painted just the same, violet with purple trim, though there were birdhouses in the miniature trees out back, which the B and B doesn't have. The inside was different from the Bric-a-Brac—the third floor was an attic instead of an apartment, and there weren't as many bedrooms—but some of the details were the same. There was a window seat on the first floor and the kitchen sink was under the back window, same as the B and B. Instead of a front porch with four white rocking chairs, like the B and B had, there was a back porch, with four different-colored chairs.

Nanu popped her head into the front room to see what I was doing. "Ah, spending some time with the Gingerbread House, are you?" she said. "Your father used to love that old thing."

I almost jumped out of my skin, I felt so excited. Nanu had called the dollhouse the Gingerbread House—the same place Dad had said "the real treasure" was.

But what kind of treasure could fit into a dollhouse? Nothing very big, and nothing that would need a big old key to unlock.

I looked carefully in each room, starting with the attic and working my way down, searching for treasure. It was more interesting than I remembered it being, now that I was looking so carefully—there was lots of furniture with lots of details, like a little pillow and blanket on each bed, and tiny clothes inside the drawers of doll-sized dressers, and a framed painting of a tree full of birds hanging over the fireplace.

But as far as I could tell, there was no treasure hidden in the dollhouse.

I got another muffin and sat next to Moneypenny on the window seat. Nanu had called the dollhouse the Gingerbread House, but there wasn't any treasure in it. But Dad had said there *was* treasure in the Gingerbread House. Either Dad was lying, or I had a real puzzle on my hands. I was beginning to think that spending the summer with Nanu was looking a little bit better, if every morning was going to start out like this, with muffins and hot chocolate and mysteries.

Then everyone got up and left except me and Nanu, and they all left their dirty dishes and cups right there on the tables.

"Well," said Nanu, eyeing all the dishes, "good thing we have four hands between us."

Running a B and B isn't all muffins and hot chocolate, it turns out.

Nanu took pity on me, though. After we'd carried

all the dishes into the kitchen she said, "Why don't you go work on the shed for a little while? Later on, maybe you can help me refresh the guest rooms."

I didn't wait for her to change her mind. I was out the back door and across the backyard faster than you could say Moneypenny, who followed along at a much more leisurely pace.

I think our bubble adventure that morning must have given her some extra pep, because usually Moneypenny only went outside if someone was dragging her. She sniffed around for a little while by the bureau I'd pulled out of the shed, but then she flopped in the shade of a tree near the fig-leaf-covered back wall and fell asleep.

The first thing I did when I was inside the shed (after I turned on the light and checked for spiders) was pull the key out of my pocket to inspect it. Sure enough, when I turned the key upside down, the shapes I saw definitely looked like two *W*s. It was my dad's, I was sure of it. I decided to put the doll-house out of my mind and concentrate on the key instead. I looked around the dusty, shadowy shed. Maybe the thing the key unlocked was in here somewhere. I put the key back into my pocket and got to work.

I checked on Moneypenny a little while later, when I was setting an old lamp next to the chest of drawers. I decided to make three piles out of all the stuff: things to keep, things to sell, and things that were broken. So far the broken pile was the biggest. Lots of cracked plates and rusted old-fashioned tools that didn't look like they'd even work anymore and dusty folded-up blankets full of moth holes. The sell pile had three lamps that maybe worked and a little side table and a bunch of chipped plates and cups, as well as the dresser where I found the key. I was trying not to put much stuff in the keep pile, because I wanted the shed to be empty when I was done.

Moneypenny was still sleeping, and her short little legs were twitching like she was dreaming about running, or maybe swimming. I squatted down next to her in the shade. "What are you dreaming about, Moneypenny?"

"Meow."

I'd know Matzo Ball's meow anywhere. I looked around and then up. He was sitting in the window of my bedroom, watching me watching Moneypenny.

"Don't be jealous, Matzo Ball!" I said, but he hopped down from the window and disappeared.

"Who's Matzo Ball?"

It was the Captain, coming through the back door into the yard, and she tilted the brim of her hat as she stepped into the sun. She was holding a fresh cup of coffee, and she had a pair of binoculars strung around her neck.

"My cat."

"Ah," said the Captain. "*Felis catus.*"

I couldn't tell if she was being serious or not. "Is that a real thing?"

"I never joke about science."

"Are you a scientist?"

The Captain nodded. "Ornithologist."

I nodded back.

"Do you know what that means?"

"Yes," I lied.

"Mm," said the Captain. She took a sip of her coffee. "Well, I'll leave you to your work."

Before she left, she scanned the line of trees on the far side of the fence like she was looking for something. I looked where she looked. There was a flutter in the trees, squirrels maybe, or birds.

I worked for a little while longer, but I didn't find anything interesting and all the dust was making me sneeze. So when Moneypenny woke up and wandered back into the house, I pulled the tarp over the piles I'd made and followed.

"Just in time," said Nanu, wiping her hands on her apron.

"For lunch?"

"For refreshing the guest rooms," she said.

The memory of hot chocolate and muffins was quickly fading.

As we walked through the main floor of the house, I looked at every keyhole. There was one on the tall skinny grandfather clock, but a little golden key was in it. There was one on the tall cabinet in the sitting room, the one where games and puzzles were stored, but that one was too small for my key, and anyway the doors were open a crack already.

I trudged up the stairs behind Nanu. She opened a closet near the end of the hall—no keyhole—and pulled out a rolling cart. It was loaded with towels and cleaning supplies and toilet paper.

First she went to the Lovebirds' Lookout. "Always knock first," she said, so I did.

No one answered, so Nanu fished a ring of keys out of her apron pocket and flipped through them until she found the one marked "LL." All the keys on her ring were regular looking, not big and interesting—that meant my key probably didn't open one of the guest rooms.

Refreshing a room is as boring as it sounds. We made the bed and fluffed the pillows and opened the curtains and put new towels in the bathroom. When we were done, Nanu locked the door and we moved on to the Romantic Retreat.

The last room was the Captain's Cove. "When your father was young," Nanu said, "he liked to work in this room if no guests were staying in it. It has the best light." Then she opened the door and went in, rolling the cart ahead of her, and I followed. She went straight to the windows to open the curtains, but I stopped by the desk. There was a big stack of books on one end and a long, colorful map of Marble Island right in the center. And underneath all the books and papers was one big pullout drawer . . .

With a big old-fashioned keyhole that looked an awful lot like the shape of my key. If this room had been where my dad liked to study, then maybe this had been his desk. And Hans had said that my dad had been a curious kid. I started imagining the curious stuff that could be hidden inside it . . . maybe something that had to do with all the things Hans said Dad used to carry around in his pockets. Or maybe there was something that would explain the Gingerbread House. A map, starting at the dollhouse and leading to treasure at the end?

"Rats," said Nanu, rustling through the cart. "I'm all out of hand towels. I'll get some from the laundry room and be right back."

This was my chance! Quick as a flash, I fished the key out of my front pocket and tried to fit it into the lock.

The key was too big. I scrunched my face in disappointment and sighed.

I meant to slide the key back into my pocket, but I missed. It clattered to the floor, and I dropped down, too, scrambling under the desk. Where did it go? It couldn't have just disappeared!

Then I heard Nanu coming up the steps. One step, another step, another. She'd be here any moment! I felt around on the floor, behind the desk legs.

Here came Nanu's footsteps down the hall. I was almost out of time and then—the very tips of my fingers caught the edge of the key.

But then I heard Nanu turn the doorknob, and I panicked. If she saw me with the key, she might take it away. After all, she *had* told me to tell her if I found anything special. I popped up to my feet, leaving the key on the carpet beneath the desk.

Nanu stopped in the doorway and looked at me. "Harriet?" she asked. "What are you doing by the Captain's desk?"

"Um," I said. I glanced down at the book on top. It was called *Perching Birds of Marble Island*. And then I noticed that someone had circled a bunch of spots on the map and made scratchy notes down one side of it, along with a little drawing of a bird. "Figuring out what an ornithologist is."

12

Island Loggerhead Shrikes

"THE CAPTAIN IS HERE FOR the whole summer," Nanu told me after she'd shooed me out of the room and locked the door. "This year, she's keeping track of our island loggerhead shrikes."

"Island loggerhead shrikes?" I said. "What the heck are island loggerhead shrikes?" I was a little bit curious, but mostly I was thinking about my key, locked now in the Captain's room. My pocket just didn't feel the same without it. It felt empty.

"They're a sort of bird," Nanu said. She rolled the cart back into the closet and shut the door. "They're threatened."

"What's threatening them?"

She wiped her hands on her apron and headed back downstairs. "Why don't you ask the Captain at teatime?"

"Island loggerhead shrikes," I said. It was fun to say, and it took my mind off my lost key a little bit. I said it all day long.

"Island loggerhead shrikes," I said as I combed the tangles out of Matzo Ball's fur.

"Island loggerhead shrikes," I said as I took Moneypenny for a walk around the block. We saw two cats on our walk—one, an orange tabby sleeping on a front porch, and the other, gray-and-black striped, crouched underneath a golf cart across the street, staring at us with shiny green eyes.

Around the corner and up the block behind the B and B, there was, I noticed, a curiously

overgrown house. Actually, this house looked a little bit like the Bric-a-Brac, like they were cousins
or something. It had the same pointy roof and the
peaks of the house had the same sort of curlicues in
the woodwork. But unlike the Bric-a-Brac, it didn't

have a front porch, and it wasn't painted interesting colors. It looked sort of run down, and the plant that grew all over Nanu's back fence—the creeping fig—was climbing over the side gate of this house, and up the side of the house too. If no one stopped it, soon the creeping fig would take over the whole place! I stopped and stared, trying to peer through the windows. I wondered who lived inside.

Later, I helped Nanu set out the tea things—pretty plates painted with flowers, little cups with fancy handles, a big bowl full of ripe red strawberries, a tall silver tea tray with three tiers. The top was loaded with scones; the middle one with finger sandwiches; the bottom one with pastries.

"Finger sandwiches, blech," I said to Moneypenny, who watched from her spot by the front window.

"For the third time, there are no fingers in the sandwiches, Harriet," Nanu called from the kitchen.

I knew there were no fingers in the sandwiches. I'd helped make them. But still.

Then Nanu came out from the kitchen, carrying a teapot in each hand. "Hot hot hot," she warned, setting them down on little metal pads she called trivets.

The newlyweds wouldn't be coming for tea; they were on an all-day excursion to see the interior of the island. Little Mateo and Big Mateo came in first, stinking of fish and sunscreen. Luckily they went upstairs to wash off before tea, and when they came back down they only smelled of soap.

Finally, in came the Captain, binoculars strung around her neck. She took off her hat when she came through the door and ran her hand across her bushy gray hair.

"Hello, lass," she said to me. She hung her hat and her binoculars on the hat rack.

"Hi," I said. "Do you want me to take your stuff up to your room? You could give me your key and

I'll take your things up there and come right back down."

"Still tip trolling, are you?" said the Captain.

"No," I said. "You don't have to give me a tip or anything."

The Captain looked suspicious, so I shoved my hands in my pockets and whistled to distract her.

Thump, thump. Moneypenny's tail beat against the window seat cushion.

"Hello, lass," the Captain said to Moneypenny, and she patted her on the head.

Then, to make her extra not-suspicious, I said, "Captain, what's threatening the island loggerhead shrikes?"

"O-ho," she answered. "That's the million-dollar question, isn't it?"

Nanu must have seen how excited that made me because she quickly said, "That's just an expression, Harriet." And then she said, "Have a scone, Captain. They're your favorites today—cranberry."

"Don't mind if I do," said the Captain. She tucked a napkin into her collar and picked up one of the pretty little plates. Nanu used the silver tongs to place a scone on it and followed that with a dollop of clotted cream on the side, and some olallieberry jam.

"So," said the Captain, taking her tea and her snack to one of the big flowery chairs in the parlor room, "do we have a budding ornithologist in our midst?"

"No," I said. I sat down in the chair across from her. Between us was a little wooden table, and the Captain set her plate on it. "I just want to know about the island loggerhead shrikes." Out of the corner of my eye I saw Matzo Ball sneaking down the staircase. I'll bet he was hoping for some of the clotted cream.

The Captain took a big bite of her scone. Crumbs rained down, and I could see why she'd tucked in that napkin. "The scones are excellent as always,

121

Agnes," she said to Nanu, before she turned to me. "Long before this place was named Marble Island, the shrikes only had to worry about their natural predators, including foxes and hawks, who think shrikes are delicious. Then, years ago, grazing animals like buffalo and goats were brought to the island on ships. Their herds have grown, and they eat up the grasses the shrikes live in, ruining their habitat. And on top of all that—the foxes and the hawks and the buffalo and the goats—two of the shrikes' very fiercest threats are right here in this house."

"Here?" I looked around at the B and B. There were lots of comfy chairs and wooden tables and stacks of books and lace doilies everywhere, but I couldn't see anything that could be dangerous for a bird. "You're lying," I said.

I felt the brush of Matzo Ball's tail against my leg as he skulked closer. He was trying to get to the cream on the Captain's plate.

The Captain shook her head and set down her scone. Her face was deadly serious. "I never lie," she said.

"Then where are the threats?" I said, crossing my arms.

"Well, you and me, for one," she said, sipping her tea. "Humans. Going hiking and not staying on the trails, stomping around and scaring off the shrikes' prey, messing up pretty much everything."

"Oh," I said. "Well, you said there were two threats here. Where's the other?"

Matzo Ball fished a paw up the side of the little table, aiming for the cream.

But the Captain was faster. She picked up her plate. "Ah," she said. "There's the little predator in the flesh. Or should I say, in the fur?"

13

Another Mystery

"MATZO BALL CAN'T BE A threat to your birds!" I said. I scooped him up. "He just got here yesterday!"

"Mrow," said Matzo Ball. He sounded insulted.

The Captain laughed. She reached over and scratched Matzo Ball's head. "It's not your cat in particular," she said. "It's *cats* in general. This island has a real cat problem, you know."

I didn't know that. "How can cats be a problem? Cats are the best!"

"In moderation, perhaps. But Marble Island has a feral cat problem."

"What's a feral cat?"

"It's a housecat that lives in the wild. There are loads of them here on the island. And cats, if they're not kept indoors, like to catch and eat other animals. Like mice, and lizards, and birds."

"Poor kitties!" I said. I rubbed my chin into Matzo Ball's fur. I couldn't imagine if my sweet boy had to live outside. Who would comb the tangles from his fur? How could he get a good night's sleep if he didn't have a pillow? The whole thought of it made me squeeze Matzo Ball a little tighter. "Come on, Matzo Ball," I said. "Let's go get you a scoop of clotted cream."

After his cream, and after all the guests had finished their tea and gone upstairs or outside, Matzo Ball decided he might want to take a little nap in the sun. And it wasn't his fault if the sunniest spot happened to be right where Moneypenny was already lying, on the big striped cushion in the window seat. And cats have claws for a reason! I'm sure Matzo Ball wasn't trying to hurt Moneypenny. He was just trying to get her attention, that's all. But sometimes Matzo Ball doesn't know his own strength.

"Matzo Ball, stop!" I called, but it was too late. He batted Moneypenny's nose with a sharp-clawed paw, and Moneypenny woke with a yip and a yowl.

"Harriet!" said Nanu. "What is that terrible noise?"

"It was just an accident," I said, scooping up Matzo Ball.

"Well, tell that cat of yours to leave poor Moneypenny alone. Maybe you'd better take him back upstairs."

"Come on, Matzo Ball," I muttered. "We know where we're not wanted."

On my way upstairs, I stopped on the second floor and stood outside the Captain's door. I raised up my hand to knock. I almost didn't have the nerve. But then I did.

The Captain opened the door. "Hello again, lass," she said. "I don't need any ice."

"I know." Matzo Ball squirmed in my arms. "Actually," I said, "I think I maybe left something in here earlier. When I was helping Nanu refresh your room."

"Ah," said the Captain. I craned my neck around her to look for the key under the desk. But the Captain stepped in front of me and held out her hand. "Is this what you're looking for?"

It was the key.

Before she could change her mind, I snatched it from her palm. "Yes," I said. And before I turned to go, I added, "Thank you."

Upstairs, I closed my door and flopped on my bed. Matzo Ball skulked around the carpet, sniffing the patches of sunlight and looking for just the right place to nap. Finally, he settled down near the window where it was warmest.

I held up the key and looked at it from every angle. I traced my finger along the two *W*s. The key was longer than my palm, but it had looked small in the Captain's big hand.

Thinking about the Captain's hand made me think of Dad's hands again, and Dad. Part of me wanted to call home and talk to him. But I was still mad about him pushing Matzo Ball off the pillow and making me come to the island, and sad about him not being here.

No Dad. No Mom. Even though I had Matzo Ball, I felt all alone.

I felt sorry for myself, that sort of sad sick feeling in my stomach that made my eyeballs tingle and sting. I squeezed my eyes shut, but tears slipped out anyway. I missed my mom. I missed my dad. I missed my own room and my own house.

I didn't want to just lie there and feel sorry for myself. So I shoved the key back into my pocket and rolled off the bed. I went over to the window. From here, I could see Nanu's shed and the stuff I'd pulled out of it. I could see the creeping fig all along the back fence. And I could see the yard behind the fence, and the house it belonged to. It was the funny pointy house I'd seen on the walk with Moneypenny. Again, I found myself wondering who might live in that house. It hadn't looked like a vacation rental; maybe no one lived in it at all.

Then I saw something in the tall trees on the

other side of the wall. Something that twinkled and flashed. I squinted my eyes to try and focus, but a cloud drifted overhead, and the flashing light disappeared.

"What do you think that is, Matzo Ball?" But Matzo Ball didn't answer. He was all the way asleep.

14
Moneypenny's Constitutional

AFTER THE WEEKEND WAS OVER, Little Mateo and his dad packed up their stuff and checked out of the Bric-a-Brac. I was a tiny bit sorry to see them go. Mateo ran over and gave me a hug before they left, which was sort of nice I guess, and then he told me that he'd left his best fish in the little refrigerator in their room as a present for me.

Nanu fried it up and Moneypenny and Matzo Ball declared a truce long enough to circle around me while I ate it, hoping for scraps.

The next day the newlyweds left the island, and they left me a ten-dollar bill, which I liked a whole lot better than the fish, but which Moneypenny and Matzo Ball liked a whole lot less.

Then it was just me and Nanu and the Captain for a few days, until new guests were set to check in on Friday. That gave Nanu "a nice little break," she said.

I thought maybe that meant that we could go to the far side of the island to the swimming pool, but Nanu said that she needed a day or so "just to rest."

"It's a big job, Harriet, taking care of this place all by myself," she said, which was a little insensitive, I thought, since I'd been such a big help all weekend.

"I don't care anyway," I said, and I stomped outside to the front porch.

But it was a lie. I *did* care.

"Harriet," Nanu called out to me, "why don't

you take Moneypenny with you if you're going to take a walk."

"I'm not going on a walk," I said. But I was.

I went down the ramp and then up the block.

The sky was bright and blue. All up and down the street, flowers were practically waving their dumb colorful petals at me. It was like the whole island was bragging about how beautiful it was. I didn't want to see *any* of it.

I shoved my hands in my pockets and squeezed them into fists. I wandered around the block to go take another look at that weird pointy house. It was tall and dark like a witch's hat. It was the only place on the whole island that looked like my bad mood. I stood in front of it and stared. Its windows were dark, with all the curtains pulled closed. The little front lawn was overgrown and dry. The flower boxes in the windows didn't have any flowers in them, just dry hard dirt.

133

I liked it.

From behind me, I heard the slow familiar tap-tap-tap of Moneypenny's claws on the sidewalk. There was Nanu, walking her.

Nanu did look sort of tired. I felt sorry that I hadn't taken Moneypenny along with me. I wanted to apologize. I almost did.

But then Nanu said, "Harriet, I know you're homesick and crabby as a five-star dinner. But dear girl, there's no call for depriving Moneypenny of her constitutional."

I didn't know what "constitutional" meant, but then I saw Moneypenny squatting on a patch of lawn to pee and I figured it out.

"I didn't mean to go on a walk," I said. "It just sort of happened."

Nanu nodded. Moneypenny finished doing what she was doing and flopped at our feet like she was all worn out. The sun was so bright I just wanted to close my eyes and disappear.

"Maybe we can go to the pool tomorrow," Nanu said.

"I don't want to go anymore," I answered.

"Where do you want to go?" Nanu asked.

"Nowhere," I said. But that was a lie too. I wanted to go home.

All week, everywhere I went, I tried to find the lock the key would open.

I tried the front door and the back door of the Bric-a-Brac B&B, but my key didn't fit into either lock.

Then, even though I knew my key was too big to fit anything small, I checked every piece of furniture in the whole B and B, top to bottom, just in case. But not one thing had a keyhole big enough for the key.

I dug through Nanu's shed, looking for an old box or something mysterious. Nothing.

I stared into every room of the dollhouse until I

got so mad and frustrated that I couldn't look any-more.

At the library in town, there was a big wooden chest in the reading nook. When I saw its keyhole—big and funny shaped, just like my key—I almost jumped out of my skin, I was so excited. Dad had said that he used to come to the library every Saturday. Was there any way that his key somehow went to this chest? I tried to sneak up on the chest to check it out. But the librarian, a noodle-shaped guy named Jamal, with glasses and tall hair, saw me skulking around and came right over before I had a chance to try my key.

"O-ho," he said. "You look like a girl on a trea-sure hunt!"

"No," I said. Then, "Maybe."

"Well," said Jamal, pushing open the chest's lid—it wasn't even locked!—"These are prizes for readers. Want to join our summer reading pro-gram?"

The chest was full of little plastic toys and bags of jacks and rubber balls and stickers.

"That's not treasure," I said.

"I suppose that's a matter of opinion," Jamal said. Then he signed me up for the summer reading program and made me a library card. He laminated it and everything, so I had no choice but to take it and say "Thank you."

I wandered around the kids' section, pulling random books off the shelves, flipping them open, reading a page or two and then putting them back. None of them seemed really interesting to me. Our library at home was way bigger and better than the island library. Being here reminded me that going to the library was something Dad and I usually did together. I was feeling especially mopey when I flipped open the cover of a book and saw something surprising. Glued to the inside cover was a little sheet of paper with a list of all the people who had checked out the book, along with the date they had checked it out.

That wasn't the surprising part. The surprising part was seeing my dad's name printed on the sheet. My dad had checked out this book, almost thirty years ago! I closed the book to look at the cover.

The Big Book of Little Things

I liked holding a book that my dad had held when he was a kid. I checked it out, along with three other books, and carried them back to the Bric-a-Brac, feeling the weight of the key in the front pocket of my overalls.

But I still felt mopey, even with the key, even with the book.

A key that doesn't have a lock to open is a pretty sad thing, if you ask me.

I sort of wanted to ask Nanu for help, but then I'd have to admit that I'd taken the key from the shed and hadn't told her about it. Maybe she'd be mad. Or disappointed. So I had no choice but to keep searching all on my own.

If I were a real detective, or a spy, I'd find a clue that would lead to another clue, and that would lead to a solution. But I wasn't a detective or a spy. I was just Harriet, and I was all alone.

15

Inside Sounds and Outside Sounds

BY THE TIME WE'D BEEN at the B and B for almost a full week, Matzo Ball was starting to feel pretty comfortable. He was doing all his cutest kitty things, like hopping onto the open door of the dishwasher to lick butter off the butter knives and finding the very comfiest spots to give himself a tongue bath.

Personally, I thought that anything Matzo Ball wanted to do was adorable, but Moneypenny didn't seem to agree. In fact, the comfier Matzo Ball got, the more upset Moneypenny got.

"Leave him alone, Moneypenny," I told her when she tried to shove Matzo Ball out of the dishwasher.

"Mind your own business, Moneypenny," I told her when she tried to get involved in Matzo Ball's tongue bath.

"Don't be so selfish, Moneypenny," I lectured when Matzo Ball tried to share the best sun patch in the front window.

"The old girl is used to her space," the Captain observed from her seat in the rocking chair. She was reading one of her bird books. "It's not always easy to make room for new things, if you're set in your ways."

I narrowed my eyes at her. "You *are* talking about Moneypenny, right?"

"Your grandmother told me that your family

is expecting a new baby soon," the Captain said, which wasn't an answer to my question, but sort of was.

"I don't want to talk about that." I turned back to Moneypenny and Matzo Ball. Matzo Ball only had a little fragment of the sunny spot on the cushion, but he was making the most of it. Moneypenny was watching him with big sad eyes.

"I'll bet that given some time, Moneypenny will learn to love your Matzo Ball," the Captain said.

"Well," I said, "Matzo Ball is a fluffy perfect angel. Anyone who doesn't know *that* is just plain wrong."

"Exactly," said the Captain.

"Babies are different, if that's what you're hinting at," I said.

The Captain smiled and put up her hands like she was surrendering. "You're way too smart for me, lass. Can't pull the wool over your eyes."

On the window seat cushion, Moneypenny groaned and rolled over onto her back. Her paws flailed around, knocking into Matzo Ball, who hissed and jumped down, slinking into the dining room and out of sight.

"Moneypenny," I said. "I know you did that on purpose."

Moneypenny just sighed and flopped over the whole cushion, relaxing now that she had the window seat to herself.

I looked past her and outside. It was a blustery day. Leaves tumbled down the street, and a man who was walking by held his hat to his head with one hand.

I went and got the stack of books I'd checked out from the library, and then I flopped down on the big flowery rug in front of the fireplace. It was way too warm right now for a fire, but I thought for a minute about how cozy it would be in the winter,

with a crackling fire and maybe some hot chocolate and a blanket.

I wouldn't be here in the winter. I'd be home with Mom and Dad . . . and the new baby. Blech.

Nanu came into the room with her craft bag and sat on an armchair. She pulled out her things and went to work on the doily she was crocheting for the back of the couch. There were doilies all over the Bric-a-Brac.

"Why do you make so many of those things?" I asked.

"Art is its own reward," Nanu said, whatever that meant.

The room was quiet except for the sound of the wind outside. It even woke up Moneypenny, who sniffed at the window. Her nose left a long, wet smear across the glass.

"The wind sure is loud today," I said.

"Actually," said the Captain, "the wind itself doesn't make a sound."

"Yes, it does," I said. "I can hear it."

"What you hear," said the Captain, "is the sound of the wind brushing up against objects, or making objects brush against one another. Houses and trees, mostly."

"You mean if there wasn't any stuff, the wind wouldn't make any sound at all?"

"Exactly," said the Captain.

"I don't believe you," I said.

But the Captain said, "I never joke about science."

I didn't know what to say to that. So I ignored it. I turned my attention to the stack of books, searching through them for the one my dad had checked out when he was a kid. I opened the cover and found his name again, on the little piece of paper glued inside. I traced my finger over his name, Walter Wermer, and I had to gulp down a big lump of feelings in my throat, feelings about missing him. I realized I wasn't mad at him anymore, just sad. I squeezed my eyes tight until they stopped tingling, and when I opened them again, I flipped through the book. It was all about little things that people make: there was a section about dioramas, and another section about shadow boxes, and one on fairy gardens, and one about making tiny books, and a great big section in the back all about doll-houses.

My brain started tingling. It was like an answer was about to pop into my brain, if I could just sit still long enough to let it.

But the phone rang sharply, breaking my concentration, and Nanu said, "Harriet, how about you answer that? And remember the way I taught you!"

The phone was in the kitchen, hanging on the wall. It was bright pink and had a long curly bright-pink cord that I liked to wind around my finger.

I picked up the phone receiver on the third ring. "Thank you for calling the Bric-a-Brac B&B! This is Harriet speaking. How may I help you?"

"Hello, sweet girl."

It was Mom.

"Hi," I answered. I wound the cord around my finger.

"Nanu's got you on phone duty, huh?"

"I guess so," I said. It was weird—I'd been thinking about Mom and Dad all day, but now that Mom was on the phone, I didn't know what to say.

"How's Matzo Ball?" she asked.

I shrugged, but then I realized that she couldn't see me so I said, "I don't know. He's okay, I guess."

"Are he and Moneypenny getting along?"

"Sort of," I said. "Not really." I stretched the cord across the kitchen as I walked to the hallway and the back door.

"We sure do miss you, Harriet," Mom said. "How are you doing? What have you been up to?"

If my throat wasn't getting all thick again, I maybe would have told Mom about the Ginger-bread House and the key, about the shed and my questions about hidden treasure. Or maybe I would have told her how much I missed her and Dad, and how mad I'd been feeling about everything.

But I couldn't squeeze any words out of my throat. I was feeling all hot and stuffy, so I cracked open the back door to feel the wind. I breathed in the fresh air. Mom was still on the other side of the phone line, waiting for me to answer. I started feeling better, like maybe I could talk without crying. Maybe I could tell Mom I missed her, and maybe I could ask her to put Dad on the phone, so I could tell him I missed him too.

Just then, there was a loud sound—*crash!*—and from the front room I heard Nanu call out, "Oh, my!"

"Mom," I said, racing back through the kitchen to see what happened, "I've got to go. I'll call you later."

I hung up the phone and ran into the front room. Nanu and the Captain were standing by the front window staring outside.

"What happened?" I asked.

"The wind blew down a big branch," said the Captain.

"It landed right on my golf cart!" Nanu said.

"Let's go take a look at the damage," said the Captain, and she and Nanu headed for the front door. I watched through the window as they went down the front steps and worked together to pull the long, heavy tree branch off the roof of her golf cart.

I don't know what happened with Moneypenny and Matzo Ball next. I think probably Matzo Ball got tired of Moneypenny always hogging the good spot, if you want to know the truth. All I know is that Matzo Ball must have snuck into the room real quietly, because the next thing I knew he was jumping up, trying to get up on the window seat, and then Moneypenny was barking and then there was just like a long flash of fur as Matzo Ball ran through the sitting room and Moneypenny chased him.

"Matzo Ball! Moneypenny!" I called, but they didn't listen.

I heard Matzo Ball's yowl and Moneypenny's

bark and I chased after Moneypenny chasing Matzo Ball straight through the dining room and down the hall and then I saw that I hadn't closed the back door all the way and the wind had pushed it open even more and Matzo Ball was heading right for it.

As soon as Matzo Ball crossed the threshold to the back porch, Moneypenny lost all interest in the chase. She turned and headed back toward the window seat. I guess she figured that as long as Matzo Ball was outside, he was someone else's problem.

Matzo Ball slowed down too. He stood in the yard sniffing the grass, his long, peachy fur swirling around in the wind. For a minute I stood in the doorway admiring him—"You're the prettiest kitty," I crooned—but then Matzo Ball caught sight of something in the tall trees on the other side of the back wall. A bird.

And then I remembered what the Captain had said about the island loggerhead shrikes, and how they were endangered, and how cats were part of the reason why.

The last thing I wanted was for my cat to prove the Captain right. "Matzo Ball," I warned, "don't even think about it!" But he totally ignored me. Tail twitching, ears vibrating, Matzo Ball took off across the yard. With one giant leap, he flew through the air. He scrambled up the climbing fig, and then he was on top of the wall, and then he was gone.

"Matzo Ball!" I clawed at the fig, trying to grab on so I could climb up after him, but the leaves pulled away from the wall.

Wait. What was this, underneath the leaves?

Close up, with my hands full of creeping fig, I saw that though most of the wall was made of bricks, one section wasn't. I pulled away more creeping fig.

One panel of the wall was made of slats of wood, banded together with strips of rusty metal.

I yanked away more fig leaves.

This part of the wall wasn't a wall at all, I realized when I saw a rusty handle. It was a door.

And on the wooden door, just above the handle, was a keyhole.

16

Behind the Door

MY FINGERS WERE SHAKING AS I reached into the front pocket of my overalls, as I grasped the key and pulled it out. I held it by its three-leaf-clover-shaped handle. I wiggled the other end, which looked like uneven teeth, into the keyhole.

The key fit. I tried to turn it.

At first, it stuck. Maybe it was too rusty to twist. I jiggled it a little bit, and then—it turned. I pushed down on the handle. And with a groan, the door swung open.

For a moment, I just stood there, blinking into the strange yard. I wasn't sure what I was seeing. The grass was tall and dry, almost up to my knees. There were three big trees in the little yard, and beneath them, it looked like little patches of air were shimmering and shining.

But then I saw that the shiny patches were actually little mirrors, hanging from almost-invisible fishing line. And the trees were full of bird feeders, too, dozens of them. And also—birds! So many birds, rustling and flapping.

I heard another sound too. A sort of gurgling coo. It was a sound I'd heard before; Matzo Ball made that sound when he saw a moth or a fly.

Or a bird.

"Matzo Ball," I said. There he was, hunkered down in the dry grass, his face turned up toward the trees. He was camouflaged, his orange-brown fur almost exactly the same color as the dry grass.

"Matzo Ball," I said again, lowering my voice

so he'd know I was serious, "don't even think about it."

Matzo Ball did more than think about it. He crouched back on his haunches, preparing to leap!

Whether these birds were island loggerhead shrikes or something else, I wasn't about to watch Matzo Ball prove the Captain right.

Matzo Ball was fast, but I was faster. He jumped, and I did too. A cloud of birds lifted off from the trees, flying up into the sky. The sound of all their wings flapping together filled my ears. Matzo Ball's orangey-brown fur filled my arms. I caught him.

He slumped and growled in annoyance.

"Nicely done, young lady," came a voice from behind me.

I turned toward the pointy house. There on the back porch stood the oldest person I had ever seen.

She was ancient. She was tall and skinny and leaned on a tall, skinny cane. Her hair—long, thin, silver—was tied into a long, skinny braid that fell over her shoulder.

Her face reminded me of the bark of a tree. It was gnarled and interesting and beautiful.

"Um," I said.

"I see you found the key," she said, nodding at the gate. I turned to look at it, Matzo Ball struggling in my arms. The key was still sticking out from the keyhole, where I'd left it.

"Where on earth was it?" she asked. "For the life of me, I couldn't find the thing."

"Um," I said again. For once, I couldn't think of anything to say. I turned to look at the woman again. She stood on her back porch among four colorful rocking chairs, all gently rocking in the wind.

"Well, young lady?" she said. "What's the matter? Cat got your tongue?" Then she laughed, loud and delightedly, at her own joke.

I heard other voices coming from the B and B.

"Harriet!" That was Nanu.

"Where'd the lass get off to?" That was the Captain.

"Um," I said, one more time. "I've got to go."

"Wait," called the woman, but I didn't. I turned and ran back through the gate, pulling it tightly closed behind me.

Back in Nanu's yard, with the neatly groomed grass and the comfortable benches and the colorful flowers, it felt almost like the whole thing had been a dream, like it hadn't happened. But the key was still sticking out of the keyhole, real as anything.

Still holding Matzo Ball, I turned the key to relock the gate. I pulled it out of the keyhole and slipped it into my pocket.

"Harriet?" called Nanu, stepping out of the Bric-a-Brac.

"Here I am," I answered, crossing the yard toward the B and B. "Matzo Ball got out of the house. But I caught him."

"That naughty boy," Nanu said.

"Did the branch ruin your golf cart?" I asked, hoping to change the subject.

"No, thank goodness," said Nanu. "Just a little dent."

We all went back inside, and this time I made sure the back door was latched. I put Matzo Ball down on the kitchen floor, and he meowed and wound himself in and out of Nanu's legs like nothing had happened at all.

She bent down to pet him. "Naughty boy," she said again.

I went straight over to the dollhouse. I needed to see something.

Yes—on its back porch were four colorful rocking chairs, just like the ones at the house behind the gate. And the little birdhouses swinging from the miniature trees . . . the house I'd visited had those too.

There's always the Gingerbread House. . . . That's where the real treasure is.

Finally, I understood: the dollhouse wasn't a model of the Bric-a-Brac B&B; it was a model of the pointy house behind us—the *real* Gingerbread House.

"Harriet," Nanu said, walking into the sitting room. "I promised Gretchen I'd bring her a crochet pattern this afternoon. Do you want to take a walk to the ice cream shop with me?"

"Yes," I said. My head felt like it was swirling with too many thoughts. A walk was a good idea. "Just . . . let me check on one thing first."

I went as fast as I could through the sitting room and up, up, up the staircase, all the way to our little apartment, and then into my room, with the door marked Harriet's Hideaway. I closed the door firmly behind me and leaned against it for a minute, breathing hard from all the stairs and all the excitement.

Thump thump, went my heart, hard and fast like the beating wings of a bird.

When I finally calmed down, I went over to the window and peered outside, over the back fence. Now that I knew what I was looking at, I could see that the little shiny patches were mirrors, swinging from the trees. From here, I couldn't see the pointy house's back porch at all. The three big trees in the yard blocked it completely.

I'd solved the mystery of the key. Now I knew what it opened.

And I'd solved the mystery of the Gingerbread House. Now I knew what it was.

But I was curiouser than ever; who was the very old lady? And why was there a door between the backyard of her funny pointy house, as funny and pointy as a witch's hat, and the Bric-a-Brac B&B? And why did the key that opened the gate have Dad's initials—*WW*? And what was the treasure hidden inside the Gingerbread House?

It seemed that every mystery I solved led to even bigger mysteries.

And I'd get to work solving these . . . right after ice cream.

17

The Gingerbread House

THE WIND WAS BEHIND NANU and me as we walked down the street toward the village. Even though it was windy, it was still a good ice cream day, nice and warm. Leaves swirled around our feet.

I glanced over at Nanu. I liked the way her curly hair danced around in the wind. I liked the way her colorful clothes waved like happy flags. I liked the way she reached over and took my hand and squeezed it. I really wanted to tell her about the key, and about the keyhole and the gate into the yard of the pointy house. But then I'd have to tell her that I'd gone through the gate without her permission. That was the sort of thing that made grown-ups upset.

I know that there are lots of kinds of lies. Back home, Dad was always telling me about all the different types of lies and why I shouldn't tell them. There's the sort of lies I usually tell, like when I convinced Dad that smoothies at Doug's Drive-Thru De-Lite were a last-day-of-school tradition, and when I told the newlyweds that my thumbs were hurt when really they weren't. Those lies are called fabrication. Then there are lies I tell when I'm embarrassed, like when I wet my bed and caused the bubble explosion and told Nanu it wasn't me. That kind of lie is called denial. I knew the name for the kind of lie I was doing now, by not telling Nanu the whole story about Matzo Ball and how I went through the gate, and even not telling her about the key in the first place. This was a lie by omission. That's when you don't tell someone something important, and you let them believe that things are different than what really happened.

The key in my pocket and the gate in the wall didn't feel like happy secrets. They felt like lies.

I snuck another glance at Nanu.

"Nanu," I said, "can I ask you a question?"

"Anything," she said, and she smiled at me. I liked the way her eyes crinkled when she smiled, which was most of the time.

"Did my dad have any bad habits when he was a kid?"

"Oh, sure," Nanu said. "Everyone has bad habits. I have a few myself!"

"You do? Like what?"

"Hmm," Nanu said. "Like sneaking sugar before real food. And staying up too late, even though I know it makes me crabby in the morning. And not hanging up my clothes! There's a big pile in my closet of things I've never gotten around to hanging."

That wasn't the sort of thing I meant. Maybe Nanu could tell from the expression on my face, because she said, "Well, all of those things really only affect me. If I eat too much sugar, I feel sick. If I stay up too late, I have a rough morning the next day. If I don't hang up my clothes, I'm the one who has a wrinkly dress. Maybe you mean things that affect other people."

I nodded. "Yes. That's what I mean."

"Well," said Nanu. Her hand was warm and dry, like the wind. "When I was a little kid, I used to steal."

I felt my eyes get wide. "You *did*?"

Nanu nodded. "I'm not proud about it, but it's true."

"What did you steal?"

"Let's see," said Nanu. "I remember one day at school, when I was younger than you are now, I took another girl's pencil."

"Her *pencil?*"

"Mm-hmm. It might not sound like much, but yes. I took her pencil."

"Didn't you have your own pencils?"

"I did," said Nanu. "I had several."

"Then why did you take hers?"

"I took her pencil," said Nanu, "because she had beautiful handwriting, and mine was terrible."

"Oh," I said.

Nanu laughed. "I think I thought that maybe if I had her pencil, I'd be able to write as well as she did. Or maybe if she *didn't* have that pencil, her handwriting would get messy, like mine."

"It didn't work, did it?"

"No," said Nanu. "It didn't work. All that

happened was that I felt terribly guilty about stealing her pencil."

"Did you give it back?" I asked.

"I wanted to," Nanu said. "I really did. But I was afraid."

I understood. "You were afraid she'd be mad at you, and you'd get in trouble."

"Yes," said Nanu. "So instead of giving her back the pencil, I threw it in the fireplace at home."

"Did it burn?"

She nodded. "It did."

I pictured a yellow wooden pencil thrown into a fire. I pictured it burning up. It wouldn't take very long, I'd bet.

"I've never told anyone about that pencil," Nanu said. "Not until right now."

I thought about that stolen pencil. About how Nanu had thrown it into the fire. About how she felt after.

"What about my dad?" I asked. "What were his bad habits?"

"Oh-h," said Nanu. "I think it might be best if you asked him that yourself."

We had arrived at Hans & Gretchen's Ice Cream Parlor. There was its green Dutch door and its little thatched roof and its window boxes full of flowers. A little family came out of the ice cream shop, and they held open the Dutch door for us to go inside.

Behind the counter, Hans was washing the ice cream scoop. He was wearing his green apron over a clean white shirt, the sleeves rolled up to the elbows. I was glad to see him. I wanted to ask him more questions about the things my dad used to carry in his pockets. I had a theory.

"Well, look who the wind blew in!" Hans said with a big smile. "Hello, Agnes. Hello, Harriet."

"Hello, Hans," Nanu said. She reached into her bag and pulled out a folded-up piece of paper. "I brought a crochet pattern for Gretchen. It smells marvelous in here, even better than usual."

It really did. It smelled warm and spicy and sugary all at once.

"Ah," said Hans. "That would be our latest creation." He gestured to a stack of fresh-baked waffle cones on the counter. "Gingerbread cones," he announced proudly. "Would you like to try one?"

I'm not a big fan of change. Usually I liked to get the exact same thing every time—two scoops of vanilla ice cream on a waffle cone. What if you try something new and it isn't any good and you're stuck with it? But the gingerbread cone smelled too good to say no to. And it seemed like a sign—a cone made of gingerbread, when I had finally found the Gingerbread House. Nanu and I both said yes. I asked for vanilla ice cream in a gingerbread cone—remembering to say please without being reminded—and Nanu got the same thing.

"Gingerbread cones," Nanu said admiringly. "What a clever idea."

"I wish I could take credit for it," said Hans.

"Was it Gretchen's idea?" asked Nanu.

Hans nodded. "We're trying them out in preparation for the big birthday—I mentioned it last time you were here. The Centennial."

"A big birthday?" I asked.

"Indeed," said Hans. "Your neighbor's. She has a very important birthday coming up, you know. One hundred years old!"

It couldn't be a coincidence—gingerbread cones and the Gingerbread House.

"Hans," I said, "are you talking about the neighbor who lives behind the Bric-a-Brac, in the tall, pointy house that looks sort of like our B and B but sort of different?"

"Sure I am," said Hans. "That's the Gingerbread House. That's where Mabel Marble lives."

Hearing Hans call it the Gingerbread House made it feel real. I really *had* found the Gingerbread House! But . . .

"Mabel . . . Marble?"

Hans nodded. "Yep. Just like the island. It's named after her family, didn't you know?"

I *didn't* know that. I'd always figured that the island was called Marble Island because it sort of looks like a marble, the way it's round and curves up in the middle. That name . . . Mabel Marble . . .

With my hand that wasn't holding the ice-cream cone, I reached into the front pocket of my overalls and pulled out the key.

I looked at the shapes that looked like letters—*WW*. And then, very slowly, I turned the key over until the letters read MM.

"Mabel Marble," I whispered. That's what the initials stood for. Not Walter Wermer.

"Harriet," said Nanu. She was so surprised that

her eyebrows shot all the way up her forehead. "Where on earth did you find that key? It's been missing for years!"

"Nanu," I said, "I want to tell you something."

"Okay," Nanu said. "I'm listening."

So I told Nanu and Hans about finding the key in the old dresser drawer in the shed. Pretty soon Gretchen came out from the kitchen to listen too. I told them about searching for a keyhole the key would fit. I told them about Moneypenny chasing Matzo Ball out of the house and across the yard, and I told them about the door in the back wall, covered over by creeping fig, and about the keyhole.

174

I told them about how the key fit it, and how I opened the door, and how I went through to the other side. I told them about the birds and the bird feeders and the bits of mirror hanging from the trees. I told them about the old lady on the back porch with her walking stick—Mabel Marble.

And the whole while I was telling the truth—the whole truth—I felt something. I felt my stomach unclenching and my heart calming and my chest opening. I felt my breaths getting deeper and my shoulders relaxing and even my toes uncurling in my shoes.

"Well," said Nanu at last. I think that is one of her favorite words. "That key has been missing for years and years. What luck that you've found it at last!"

18

Mabel Marble

NANU TOLD ME MORE ABOUT Mabel Marble and the Gingerbread House as we ate our ice cream and walked toward home.

"Mabel Marble was born right here on the island a hundred years ago," Nanu began.

"Really?" I said. "She's *really* a hundred years old?"

"She will be," said Nanu. "Her birthday is at the end of the summer. Her centennial birthday."

"Were she and her family the first people to live on Marble Island?" I asked. "Did they *discover* it?"

"Oh, no," Nanu said. "People lived on this land long before the Marbles came here. First there were the Indigenous people, who lived here for thousands of years. Then, long before the Marbles's time, Europeans came and claimed the land."

"That's not fair," I said. "How could they say it was theirs if it already belonged to someone else?"

"Excellent question," Nanu said. "It wasn't fair. But it is what happened. Unfortunately, things that aren't fair are a big part of our history, both on and off Marble Island."

I thought about that. "So how did the Marbles end up here? Were they the Europeans?"

Nanu shook her head. "Much later, after the Europeans, the United States became a country, and this island became part of California. And then there were several people who owned it. First there was a man named Albert Licker, and then two very rich brothers named Morgan and Wallace Benning. And then, finally, they sold the island to Mabel Marble's grandparents. They had two teenage sons when they moved here. One of them hated the island and moved away as soon as he turned eighteen—he longed for big-city life. And the other boy loved it here. He stayed, and got married, and he and his wife had a daughter, almost one hundred years ago."

"Mabel Marble," I said.

"Mabel Marble," Nanu said. "You know, when your dad was a kid, he didn't have the easiest time making friends. His classmates didn't always understand him. He had curious hobbies, and the other kids teased him. But he always had a friend in Mabel Marble. He used to go through that gate all the time, back and forth. Eventually he got better at making friends, and then he got busy with sports and things, but he still visited Mabel Marble from time to time."

"Nanu," I said, "did my dad like to make miniatures? Was he the one who decorated the dollhouse?"

"Oh, yes," Nanu said. "He got quite good at it for a while. He was the one who turned the dollhouse into a replica of the Gingerbread House. That was one of the things kids teased him about, actually—about playing with doll stuff."

I thought about my dad as a kid, going to the library and checking out books, taking them home to the Bric-a-Brac B&B. I imagined him wearing these very overalls, sitting at the big desk in the Captain's Cove where the light was the best, building and painting little pieces of furniture. I pictured him visiting Hans & Gretchen's Ice Cream Parlor, his pockets full of tiny paintbrushes and screwdrivers and itty-bitty nails, everything he needed to make miniatures. Nanu said that the other kids hadn't always understood my dad. That made me think about how I sometimes thought that *he* didn't understand *me*. It occurred to me that maybe I didn't understand my dad as well as I thought I did. Maybe parts of my dad were a mystery too.

By the time Nanu and I had walked back to the Bric-a-Brac, I had licked away all the vanilla ice cream down to the top of the gingerbread waffle cone. I took a bite. It was crisp and spicy and sugary and delicious.

Standing on the sidewalk, I could see Moneypenny in the window seat. And there, tucked in beside her, sharing the patch of sun, was Matzo Ball. They slept together, as calm and comfy as could be.

"Would you look at that," Nanu said.

"Tonight," I said, "I'm going to call home. I'm going to ask my dad all about being a kid on the island. I'm going to tell my parents how much I miss them. And I'm going to tell them about Matzo

Ball and Moneypenny sharing the sun."

Nanu put her hand on my shoulder. It was smaller and lighter than Dad's, but just as warm.

Nanu and I went through the B and B and out to the backyard. When we reached the back wall, we worked together to clear away the creeping fig from the door.

Then I reached inside the pocket of my overalls and pulled out the key. I put it in the keyhole and turned it.

"We'd better knock," Nanu said.

I knocked.

"Come on through," said a voice—Mabel Marble.

So I pushed open the gate.

"Hello, neighbors," said Mabel Marble. She was sitting on the back porch, rocking in a rocking chair. Her walking stick was by her side.

"Looks like my grandgirl found the lost key,"

said Nanu. We crossed the yard through the tall, dry grass.

"Watch out for gopher holes," warned Mabel Marble. "You don't want to turn an ankle."

We made our way through the grass and across the yard. Up close, I noticed that the bird feeders hanging in the trees were in the shape of little houses, decorated with seeds—black seeds for the roof; brown seeds for the walls; red seeds for the door and chimney. They looked just like little gingerbread houses, but made for birds to eat instead of people.

We went up onto the porch.

"Introductions," Mabel Marble said.

"Mabel Marble, I'd like you to meet my grand-daughter, Harriet," said Nanu. "I hear you had an informal meeting earlier today."

"Hello, Harriet," Mabel Marble said solemnly. She extended her hand for me to shake. I shook it. The skin on her hand was thin and veiny, and I could see the shape of her bones underneath. Up close, her face was even wrinklier than it had seemed before. It reminded me of the shape of the island—the hills and the ridges, the valleys and the roads.

On the ferry, Dad had said: *There's always the Gingerbread House. . . . That's where the real treasure is.*

Was this what Dad had meant? That the treasure wasn't a thing, but a person? Mabel Marble.

I felt shy. "Hello, Miss Marble," I said.

"Call me Mabel Marble," she said. "Everyone does."

"Hello, Mabel Marble," I said, grinning. It was a wonderful name.

She lifted her chin to indicate that we should sit. Just like with the dollhouse, here were four rockers, each painted a different color. She was sitting in the green one; Nanu took the purple rocker, and I chose the blue, my dad's favorite color.

"These chairs are some of the only things I kept when I sold the B and B," Mabel Marble said.

"You used to own the B and B?"

Nanu nodded. "Mabel Marble ran the Bric-a-Brac until about forty years ago. Then she sold it to Dadu and me."

"I sold the Bric-a-Brac," said Mabel Marble, "but I kept the Gingerbread House. Your father used to come through the gate from time to time, too, until the key was lost. Harriet, wherever did you find it?"

I told her about Nanu's shed, and the old dresser,

and the peeling-up paper at the bottom of the drawer, and the key beneath.

"Well," said Mabel Marble, "it sounds like that key was just waiting for you to come along and find it."

I didn't *really* believe in things like that—like fate and magic and stuff. But still . . . it sort of felt true. Like the key had been waiting for me.

"Mabel Marble," I said, "can I ask you a question?"

"Of course," said Mabel Marble.

I thought about how Dad had once said that sometimes, on hot days or days when the B and B felt too crowded, he liked to go to the basement, and how Nanu had told me that the B and B didn't have a basement.

"Did my dad spend any time in your basement?" I asked.

"Indeed he did," Mabel Marble answered. "He

liked it down there. It's nice and cool, and it's quiet. A good place to get away from it all."

"Walter always did like a secret place," Nanu said. "When he was very little, he'd slide underneath his bed to be alone, but then he got too big to fit."

"A funny thing about old keys, old locks—sometimes, a key fits more than one lock. That key, for instance," Mabel Marble said, nodding to the key in my hand. "It opens the gate, but it also opens the door to my basement! I haven't been down there in decades, due to the missing key and all the steep stairs. As far as I know, there's nothing down there but dirt and spiders. But it's been so long, who knows? Would you like to find out?"

I went down the porch stairs and around to a pair of cellar doors close to the ground. I opened them to find a flight of cement stairs, and then another door. Underneath my hair, my scalp tingled, like something great was about to happen. This door was painted black, but the paint was faded and peeling. And there was the keyhole, just the same as the one in the gate. My key fit right into it.

I pushed open the basement door. A waft of cool air spilled out, smelling like dust and darkness. I wasn't so afraid of spiders anymore. I reached into the basement and found a switch on the wall. I flipped it, thinking there was no chance the light bulb would still work after all this time. But it did. Between the light from the bulb and the light from outside, the small basement looked less spooky and more interesting.

I looked around. There was a picnic chair sitting open, and next to it was a medium-sized cardboard box. On its side in big black letters, someone had written "WALT'S STUFF." It was my dad's handwriting, only sloppier, just like in the library book. He'd written the words when he was a kid.

I picked up the box and carried it up the stairs into the sunlight. Then I set it down and crouched next to it. The first thing I saw was a whole bunch of partially finished dollhouse furniture. There were some pieces that needed painting; there was a little car with no wheels; there was a bag full of tiny books, some blank, some with scribbly lines inside.

And there was a toolbox. Inside were little paintbrushes and tiny screwdrivers and itty-bitty nails.

My dad's dollhouse stuff. And it had been sitting here, in the basement of the Gingerbread House, for all these years. I hadn't known that the key I found in Nanu's shed would lead me to my dad. I hadn't even known that I'd wanted it to.

But all over the island, the whole time I was thinking about the key and the Gingerbread House, really I had been finding my dad: His plaque for eating ice cream 211 days in a row that hung in Hans & Gretchen's Ice Cream Parlor. The book about miniatures he'd checked out from the library. His overalls, which fit me just right.

And now this box of his stuff. I knew he'd meant that Mabel Marble was the Gingerbread House treasure, but this was a treasure too—a treasure that maybe he didn't remember he'd sort of buried underground, here in the deep, dark basement, locked behind a door that no one could open until I found the key. It made me feel like my dad was sort of here, even though he wasn't.

All of a sudden, I wanted to talk to my dad. I wanted to talk to him so much that a big hard lump came into my throat and then I couldn't talk to anyone, not for a minute, until I managed to swallow it down. Then I stood, wiping dust from my overalls—Dad's overalls—and I called up to the porch, "Nanu, can you tell me Dad's cell phone number?"

Nanu smiled, but she didn't say anything except, "Of course I can."

In Nanu's kitchen, I lifted the pink phone receiver and dialed the number she'd given me. I held my breath, wondering if he would answer, but I didn't need to worry. He picked up before the second ring.

"There's my girl," he said, and then the lump was back, and this time it didn't go away until I let the tears come out. I stood in the kitchen squeezing Nanu's phone and crying, big noisy crying, and on the other end of the phone line, I heard Dad sniffing too. But it was okay, because we were together, even if we weren't.

"Dad," I said, when the lump was gone again, "I found the Gingerbread House."

"Did you?" Dad said. I imagined him on our back porch, where he liked to stand while talking on the phone. I imagined the way he grinned when something made him happy. I imagined him adjusting the bill of his baseball cap, pulling it down a little in the way he sometimes did.

"Yes. And I found your miniature stuff in Mabel Marble's basement, and the book you checked out from the island library."

"Ah," said Dad. "It's been years since I thought about those miniatures."

"They're really good," I said. "I like them."

"Thank you, Harriet," Dad said. Then he said, "I really miss you. It's just not the same without you."

I wound the pink curly cord around my finger. Why is it sometimes so much easier to say things that aren't true than to say the things that *are* true, that are the most true? At last I blurted, "I miss you too. I miss you so much."

Dad said that he'd come visit in just a few days, and that we could go through his miniature stuff together, and that he'd help me finish clearing out Nanu's shed, and I told him about the key and the letters on it and how I'd thought they'd stood for Walter Wermer before I figured out that they were for Mabel Marble instead.

But it didn't really matter what we were talking about. All that mattered was that we were talking, and that I knew that Dad understood me, and he knew that I understood him.

"Now that you've found the key," said Mabel Marble when I walked back through the gate and up to the porch, "I hope you'll use it quite often to come and visit me. I'm the last Marble, you know. I could use the company."

I sat back down in the blue chair. "The last Marble?"

She nodded. "I've lost all my Marbles," she said seriously. But then she smiled, and then she laughed. "We have to laugh at the hard things sometimes. It makes them easier to bear."

I thought about how when I'd wet the bed and made that mess of bubbles when I was washing the sheets, Nanu had laughed but I hadn't. I had gotten mad, and I'd lied and said that I hadn't made the mess.

That was something I'd have to think more about later. If I could laugh instead of getting so mad. Instead of lying. I didn't know if it would work. But maybe I could try.

Sometimes you look at a thing—like a mess of bubbles, or a summer spent away from home, or a key with letters on it—and you get stuck seeing it just one way. But maybe, like with the key—the *WW* that actually read MM—you can look at it in a different way too. It can mean something new, if you let it.

Nanu told Mabel Marble that I was going to be on the island all summer because my mom was on bed rest. And that I was a kid who had lots of energy.

"This is excellent news," said Mabel Marble. Then she asked, "Harriet, might you be interested in helping me with a few things this summer? I

could use someone with lots of energy to help make gingerbread houses for the birds. I'm not getting any younger, you know."

I looked out at the yard, at the box marked "WALT'S STUFF," full of dollhouse furniture, at the trees full of birds, at the little houses swinging from the branches. I saw the open gate, and through it I saw Nanu's funny shed and the back door of the Bric-a-Brac B&B.

I saw the edge of the window way up on the third floor, the window of my room—Harriet's Hideaway.

None of this was what I'd figured my summer would be like. I thought I'd be at home with Mom and Dad and the neighborhood kids. Yet here I was.

I could be mad about it. Or maybe I could be curious instead.

"Okay," I said to Mabel Marble.

And I knew that I was saying okay to more than just Mabel Marble. I could feel it. I was saying okay to this whole summer that I hadn't expected. I was saying okay to phone calls with Mom and Dad instead of being together at home. I was saying okay to staying here, with Nanu and the Captain and Mabel Marble and the bird feeders and the birds. After all, if Matzo Ball could find a place in the sun alongside big old Moneypenny, then I could find a place here too.

So I tucked the key back into the pocket of my overalls. Now that the key wasn't a secret, the weight of it felt good there instead of bad. I rocked in the chair. I watched the birds. In the trees, the wind chimes sang and the leaves rustled. The wind was strong.

And so was I.

Acknowledgments

It turns out that writing a mystery is hard. (Lots of fun! But hard!) I am indebted to two friends in particular who helped me sort out Harriet's story, Martha Brockenbrough and Nina LaCour. This book wouldn't be what it is without the loving attention you both gave to the manuscript.

More than ever, I am in awe of the careful, thoughtful insights of Jordan Brown, my editor and friend. The whole Walden Pond Press team has been such a warm, consistent champion for my work—Debbie Kovacs, Donna Bray, thank you both for always being so enthusiastic and supportive. I'm grateful to designer Molly Fehr, art director

Amy Ryan, Emma Meyer in marketing, and Lauren Levite in publicity. Thanks also to Lindsay Wagner for the careful copyedits, and especially to Dung Ho for your incredible cover and interior art. What a thrill it is to see Harriet and her world through your eyes!

Thanks also to Rubin Pfeffer, who always has time to talk books, and whose name is almost as fun to say as Mabel Marble's. I truly appreciate you.

Always, dearest thanks to my family of siblings—Sasha, Zak, and Mischa—as well as my own little family—Keith, Max, and Davis. I love you all.

Turn the page to start reading

Harriet Spies

by Elana K. Arnold

1

A Visitor to Marble Island

IF YOU'RE NOT A PEOPLE person, you probably wouldn't like living at a bed-and-breakfast.

(Even if you really like beds, and you really like breakfasts.)

Lucky for me, I *am* a people person . . . most of the time. I think people are interesting. They look all different sorts of ways, and they do their hair in all different sorts of styles, and they wear all different sorts of outfits. Especially when they are on vacation. And pretty much everyone who comes to my Nanu's Bric-a-Brac B&B on Marble Island is on vacation.

I'm not here on vacation, though. I'm here because my mom back home is pregnant and on bed rest, so she can't look after me, and my dad has to travel for work, so he can't look after me, either. Usually, Nanu's job is to run the B and B, but this summer her job is also to look after me. And my job is to help her with B and B stuff. And also to look after Matzo Ball, the world's best cat.

I guess Nanu's basset hound, Moneypenny, doesn't have a job, unless it's hogging the sunny spot in the front window. She's getting a little better at sharing with Matzo Ball, though.

Actually, I have lots of jobs. Besides helping Nanu with the B and B and taking care of Matzo Ball, I'm also cleaning out Nanu's storage shed and I'm making gingerbread birdhouses with Mabel Marble, the neighbor who lives on the other side of the wall in the backyard. And sometimes I help Hans and Gretchen by tasting new ice cream flavors at their shop (though vanilla is still my favorite).

My goal *was* to get the back shed all cleaned out before my dad came to visit me. But it had already been two weeks since he'd first brought me to the island and he was arriving today, and with all my other jobs, the shed still hadn't been cleaned out.

Maybe that was better, though. It meant that Dad would be able to help me. Dad likes to be helpful.

After we washed the breakfast dishes, Nanu and I got ready to go pick up Dad from the ferry. I was so excited to see him that I kept doing my Happy to See Dad dance, which I was making up as I went along. Basically it involved lots of spins and dramatic arm movements and things like that.

"If you keep that up," said the Captain, "poor Moneypenny won't ever settle in for her morning nap."

The Captain, a visiting ornithologist to Marble

Island, was Nanu's longest-standing guest at the Bric-a-Brac. (An ornithologist, if you don't know, is a bird expert. And do you know what experts love, more than almost anything else? Talking about the thing they're an expert on. Don't get the Captain going about island loggerhead shrikes if you don't have at least half an hour to listen.) In addition to being Nanu's longest-standing guest, the Captain is also the tallest. And maybe the strongest. Everything about the Captain is impressive. Now she was standing at the bottom of the stairs. She had on her birding vest, with all the little pockets, and her birding hat, with its wide brim, and she wore her binoculars around her neck. She was patting all the pockets of her vest, like she was looking for something.

"Moneypenny already had two naps this morning," I said, which wasn't technically true, but might have been. "She's all napped out."

"Hmm," said the Captain, and she looked like maybe she was going to say something else, but just then Nanu came out of the kitchen carrying a big paper bag—the kind you get from the grocery store—and held it out.

"Here you go, Captain," Nanu said. "There was just enough olallieberry jam left to make your sandwiches. And there's hard-boiled eggs, and a thermos of tea, and fruit, of course."

"Thank you, Agnes," said the Captain. Then she asked, "Have you seen my compass?"

The Captain was one of the smartest people I'd ever met, but she sure did misplace things a lot. Fortunately, Nanu was *great* at finding things. You know that saying, about how someone might lose their head if it wasn't screwed on? I don't think the Captain would ever forget her head, but she forgets most everything else. Except her binoculars. A birdwatcher wouldn't get far without those.

5

"I found the compass on the dining room table and slipped it into your lunch bag so you wouldn't forget it," Nanu said.

"Ah," the Captain said. "Thank you." She took the lunch bag. It looked heavy.

Nanu picked up her bright-yellow hat from the entry table and pushed it firmly over her curly hair. I like Nanu's hair. I hope that one day when I'm really old mine will be silver and gray and white and brown, like hers.

"Agnes," said the Captain, frowning, "your hat has so much cat hair on it that it's practically meowing." She set her lunch bag on the front table, took the hat from Nanu's head, and, opening the front door, shook it until Matzo Ball's peachy perfect fuzz rose from it in a cloud. "The fusillade of fur is really becoming a problem," she continued. "It gets everywhere. Something needs to change." She handed the hat back to Nanu.

"He barely drops any fur at all," I said, ignoring the Captain's showy big words.

Matzo Ball must have heard us talking about him. Or maybe he just heard the front door opening. Either way, he appeared like a bolt of silent orange lightning and darted outside. He stopped still, all his perfect whiskers pointing forward. Something was rustling around in the front bushes, and Matzo Ball was going to do his best to sneak up on it. He took one silent step forward . . . then another . . .

The Captain's big, square hands reached down and grabbed him, just before he leaped into the bushes. "Oh no, you don't," she said.

"Mrow," said Matzo Ball, insulted.

"He wasn't going to hurt anything," I said. "He was just *exploring*."

"Tell that to the bird I pried out of his jaws the day before yesterday," said the Captain. She carried Matzo Ball back inside and dropped him unceremoniously on the rug. I could tell from the way he twitched his ears that he was irritated, but he stretched out a leg and began to groom it, pretending that he didn't care at all about the Captain. "Harriet," she said, "I've told you at least half a dozen times that you must keep a better watch on this *feline* of yours."

I know that "feline" is just a fancy word for "cat," but it was the *way* the Captain said it that I didn't like. I dropped to my knees and scratched the top of Matzo Ball's head to distract him from the insult. "I always know exactly where Matzo Ball is," I said, which was a lie. It's basically impossible to *always* know where a cat is. They are very particular about their private time.

But the Captain wasn't listening to me. "Agnes," she said to Nanu, "I really do wonder if the cat should be allowed downstairs at all. Between the bird chasing and the shedding and the clawing, it might be better for everyone if he was kept strictly upstairs."

"It wouldn't be better for Matzo Ball." I scooped him onto my lap and squeezed his fuzzy, perfect, peachy body. He began to purr. "It wouldn't be better for *me*." I turned to Nanu. "Tell the Captain that Matzo Ball can go anywhere he wants."

But Nanu didn't. Instead, she said, "The Captain has a point, Harriet. You do need to keep a better eye on him. Cute as Matzo Ball is, his time here hasn't entirely been smooth sailing."

"If it's too much responsibility for Harriet to mind her cat," the Captain said, "maybe Walter could take him back across to the mainland."

There was no way I was going to let Dad take my cat away from Marble Island. And what made the Captain think she was in charge, anyway? She was just a guest at the bed-and-breakfast! A bossy guest.

"One way or the other," said the Captain, picking up her lunch bag, "something must be done about that cat."

I narrowed my eyes at the Captain's lunch bag. Then I said, "Nanu, did you give the Captain all the olallieberry jam? I was saving it for Dad."

"We can stop by the market for a fresh jar." Nanu put her hat back on.

I didn't really want to make jam sandwiches for lunch. I was just mad at the Captain. Sometimes when I'm mad or anxious or bored, I say things that aren't true. It's a bad habit, and one I'm trying to break. But now I had another problem, which was that I didn't want to stop at the market.

"Let's just make egg salad," I said. "I don't want to waste any of my Dad time at the grocery store."

Dad had told me on the phone that he'd only be able to stay for four hours, the time between when the first morning ferry arrived and when the early-afternoon ferry left, so that he could get home to Mom before dinner. The Captain had given me an old watch with a flashlight and a countdown timer on it, and I had it strapped to my wrist, ready to go.

All of us went out of the B and B together after I said goodbye to the pets. Moneypenny was asleep on the window seat, and Matzo Ball was continuing his tongue bath. He was surrounded by a ring of shedding fur, but I ignored it. Nanu put a sign on the door—"Back in a Jiffy!"—and the Captain walked up the street to her Jeep. I wasn't at all sorry to see her go.

Then Nanu and I climbed into her golf cart. Almost everyone who lives on Marble Island drives a golf cart instead of a regular car. The Captain has a Jeep because her job is to study the island loggerhead shrikes, a very important and very specific type of bird, and to do that, she has to drive on the bumpy dirt roads to the middle of the island to observe them. I had been asking her to take me along, but the Captain says I have to practice being quiet for thirty whole minutes—all in a row—before she will. Otherwise, I'll scare off the shrikes. That's what she'd originally given me the watch with the timer for. Practice. So far, the best I'd done was eighteen minutes and twenty-three seconds.

Nanu started up the golf cart and off we went. I was so excited to see Dad I could hardly stand it, but luckily Marble Island is pretty small, and it only took us a few minutes to get to the dock.

The ferry was already there!

"It's early today," Nanu said, approvingly. Nanu likes it when things are on time, and she likes it even better when they're early.

I jumped out of the golf cart as soon as it pulled up to the curb. A whole herd of tourists was pouring down the ramp from the ferry—a big mess of strollers and backpacks and hats and parasols and people, some pointing at a pelican who sat on the railing, some staring down at their phones as if whatever they were looking at was more interesting than Marble Island, even though they'd just arrived.

But no Dad.

"Maybe he missed the ferry," I said to Nanu, who had gotten out of the golf cart and stood beside me. "Or maybe," I said, suddenly sick to my stomach, "something is wrong with Mom and he couldn't come at all."

"Or maybe," said Nanu, bending down so our cheeks were side by side, "he's right there."

She pointed, and I looked, and there he was. Blue baseball cap and a big smile. My dad.

I ran through the herd of tourists straight for him. Dad opened his arms and I jumped up, and he caught me.

"Hey there, Harriet." His voice was sort of rough like his cheek. He squeezed me tight for a long time before he set me down, and then he put his big warm hand on my shoulder, right where it belongs.

"Hello, Walter," said Nanu. Dad hugged her, too, and then the three of us made our way back to the golf cart.

Right then, if the Captain had seen me, she would have been surprised. For once, I couldn't have said a word, even if I'd wanted to. Even though I was happy, my throat felt all tight and full, as if a bunch of words were crowding together and blocking the way, like a traffic jam. And not one of them could get through.

Some of the words were happy, but not all of them. I was glad Dad was here, but now that he

14

was, I was also mad that he would be leaving in four hours. I didn't *want* to feel mad. Nanu says that sometimes you can choose how you feel, but I don't know about that.

I set my timer for four hours and watched as the seconds started ticking away.

I swallowed down the big tangled lump of words. "Come on, Dad." I grabbed his hand and pulled him toward the golf cart. "We can't waste any time!"